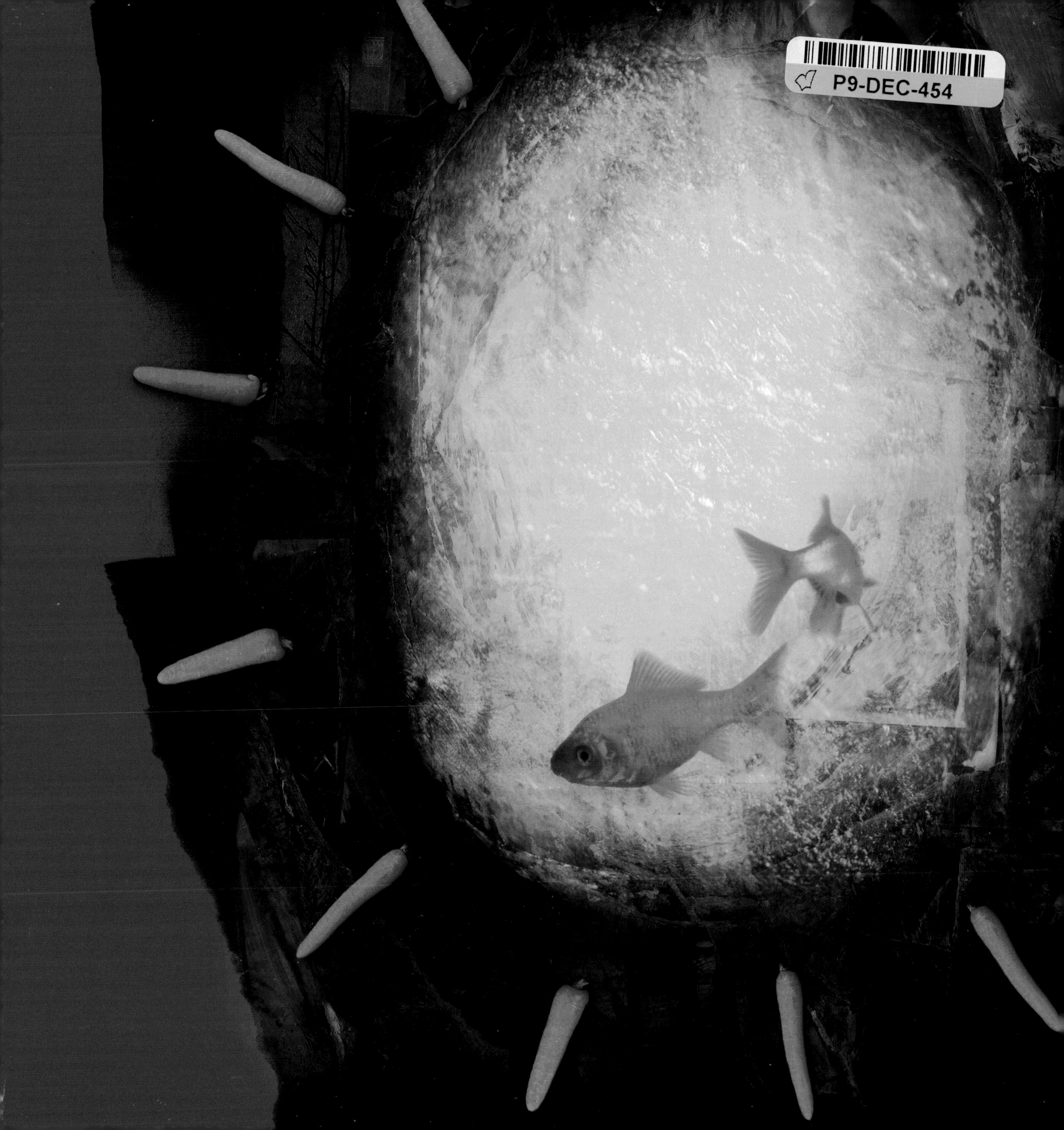

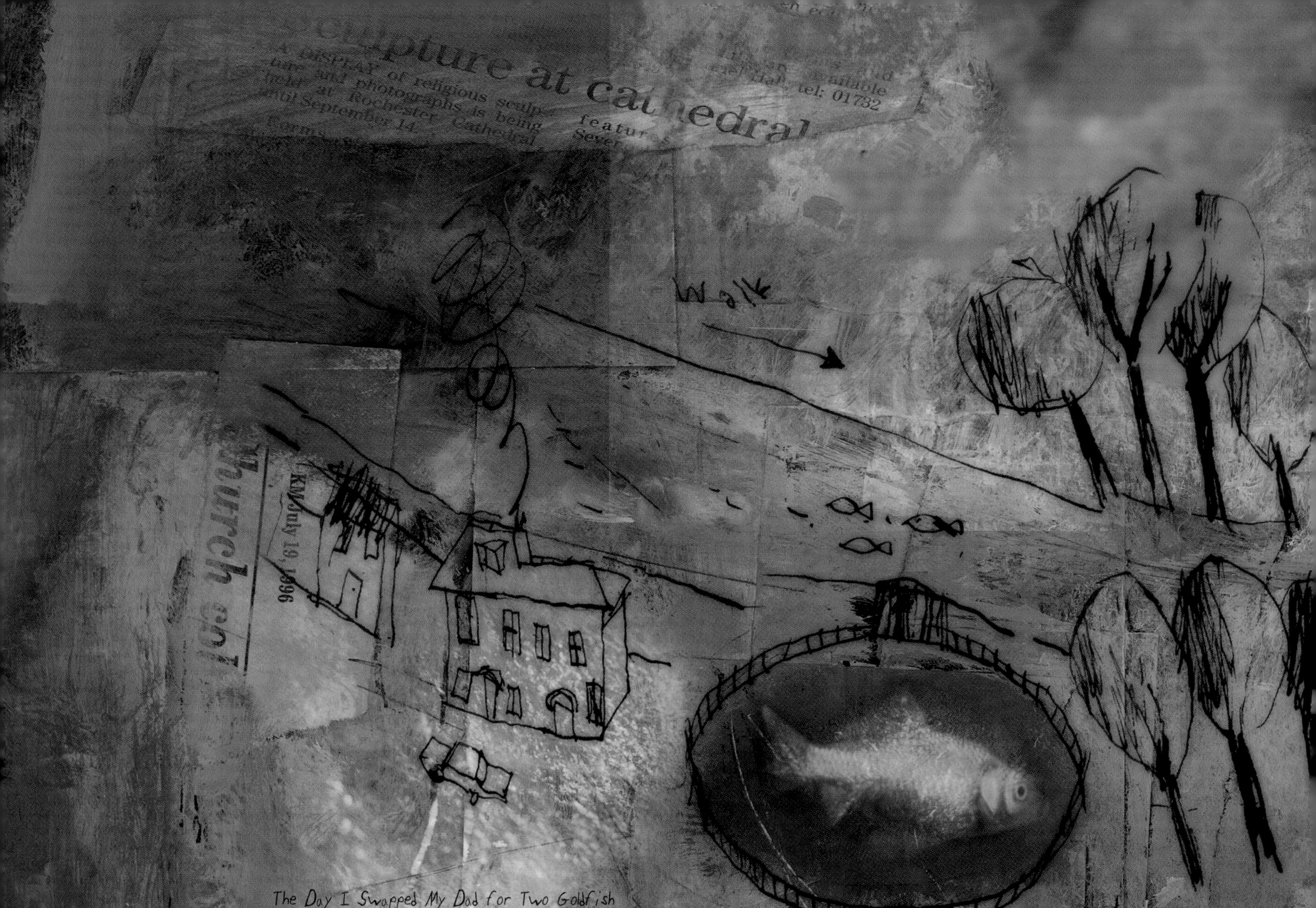
culpture at cathedral
Walk
KM July 19, 1996

The Day I Swapped My Dad for Two Goldfish

Manufactured in China by South China Printing Company Ltd.
 For information address HarperCollins Children's Books, a division of HarperCollins Publishers, 1350 Avenue of the Americas, New York, NY 10019.
www.harperchildrens.com

Library of Congress Cataloging-in-Publication Data is available from the publisher.
ISBN 0-06-058701-6 — ISBN 0-06-058702-4 (lib. bdg.)

Book design by Dave McKean @ Hourglass

1 2 3 4 5 6 7 8 9 10 ❖ Revised edition, 2004

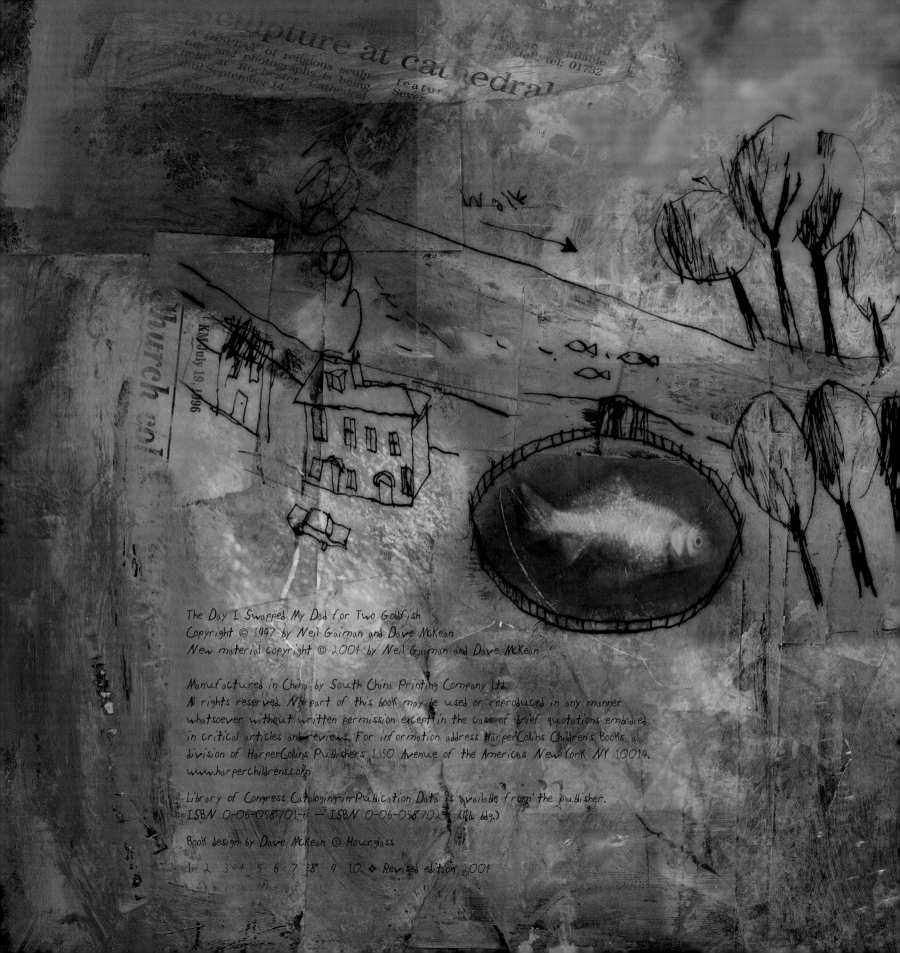

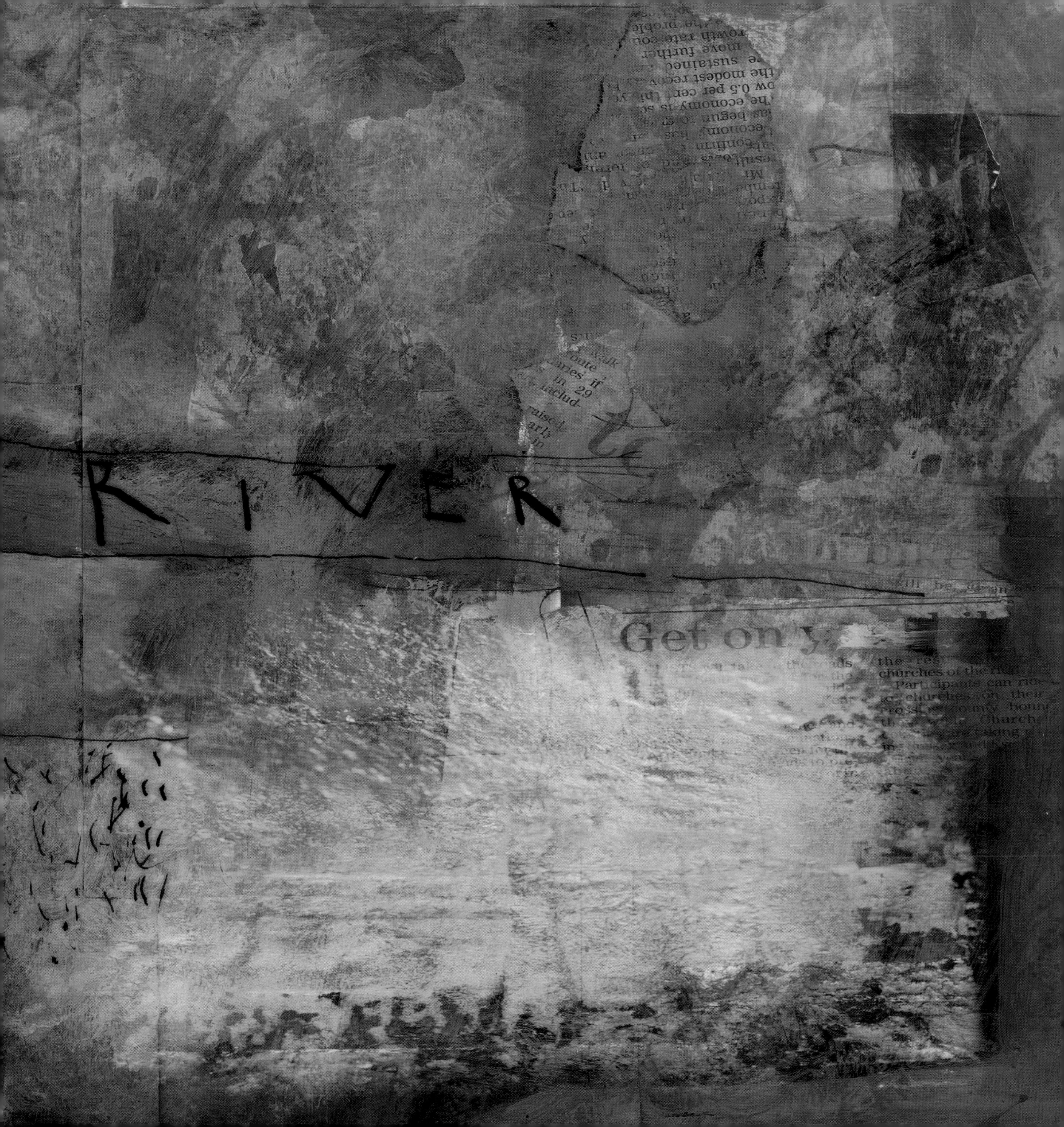
RIVER
Get on y
churches of the ri
Participants can rid

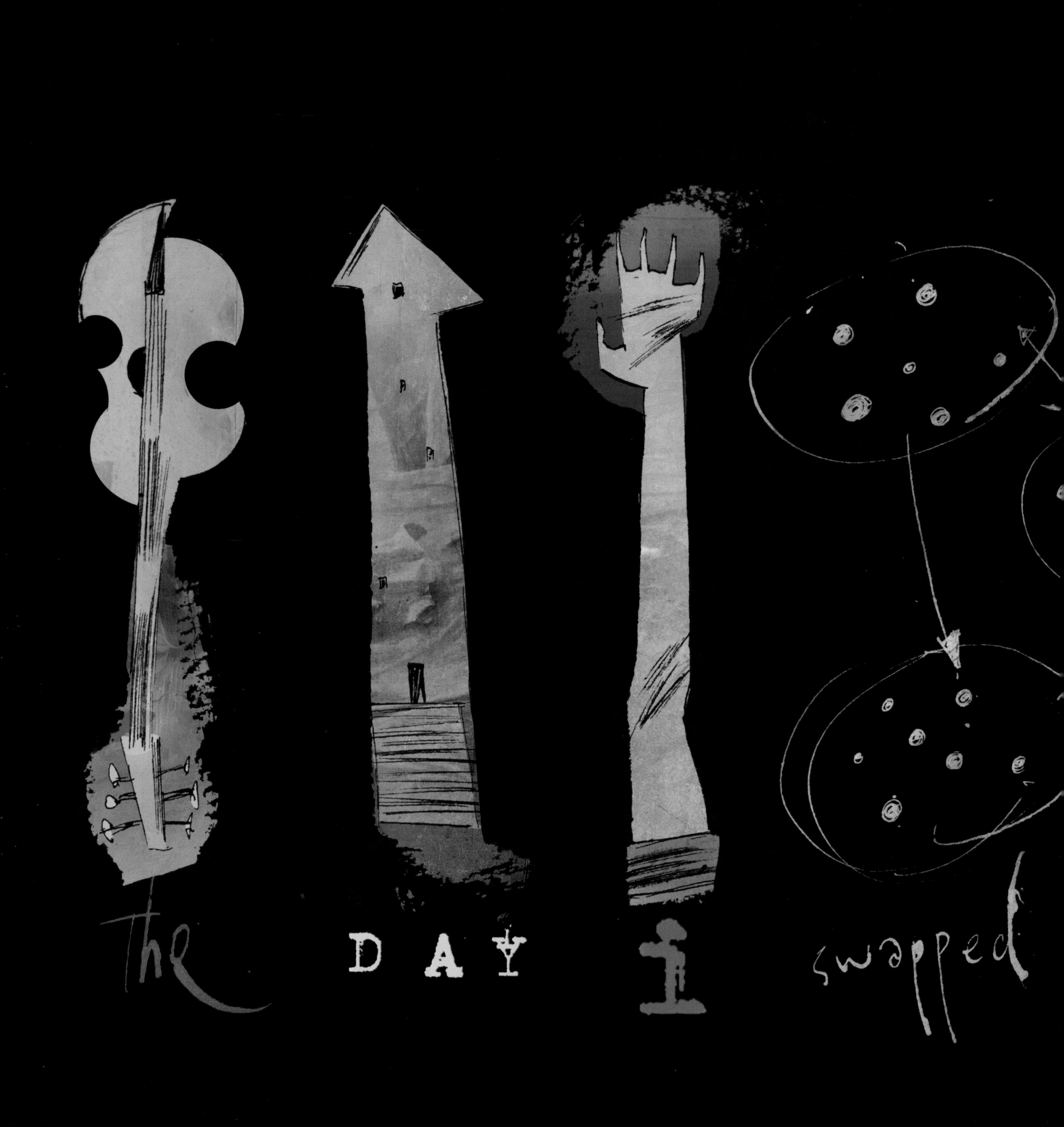
the DAY I swapped

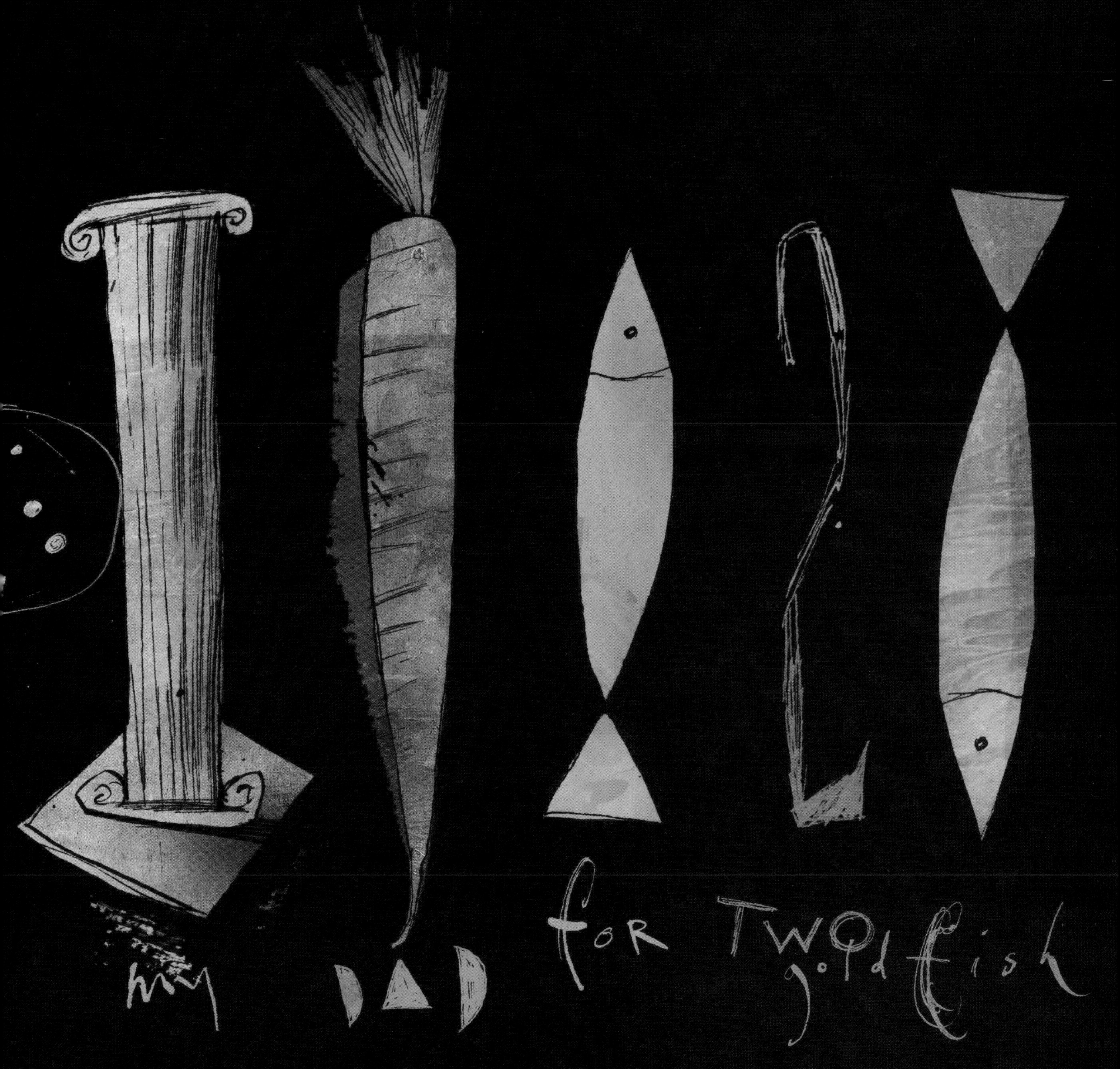
my DAD for TWO goldfish

HarperCollinsPublishers

Lost:

One book. If found, please return to Hayley Campbell
(although she may be too big for it)
or Maddy Gaiman (although it may be too big for her).
No fish, please.

Wanted:

One halibut, must be in good working order, own fins,
no skate please.
Will swap two infants, one called Yolanda, one called Liam.

Offers to Mr. David Tench McKean, Esq. c/o The Publisher.

One day my mom went out and left me at home with just my little sister and my dad.

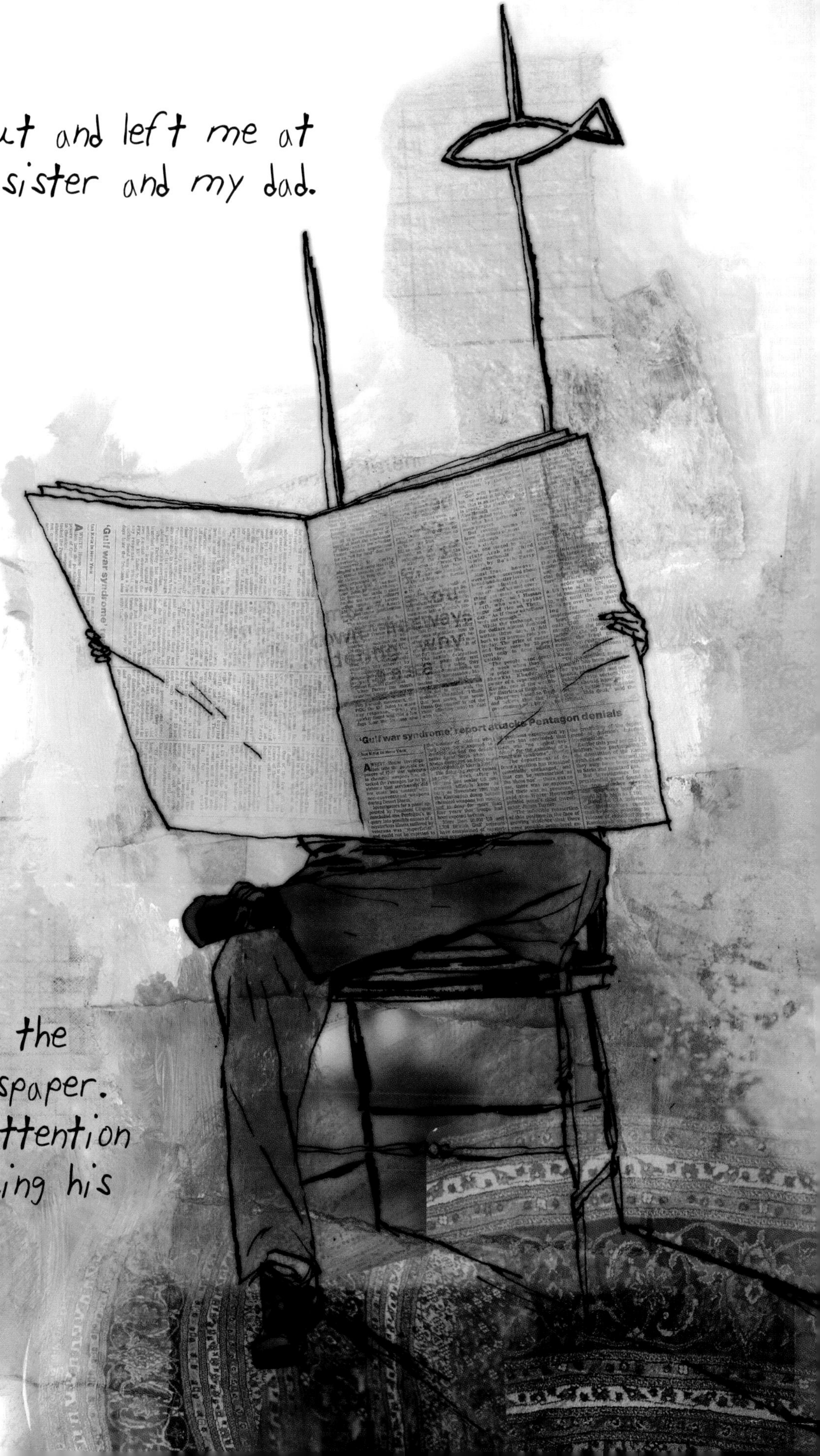
'Gulf war syndrome' report attacks Pentagon denials

My dad sat in front of the television, reading his newspaper. My dad doesn't pay much attention to anything, when he's reading his newspaper.

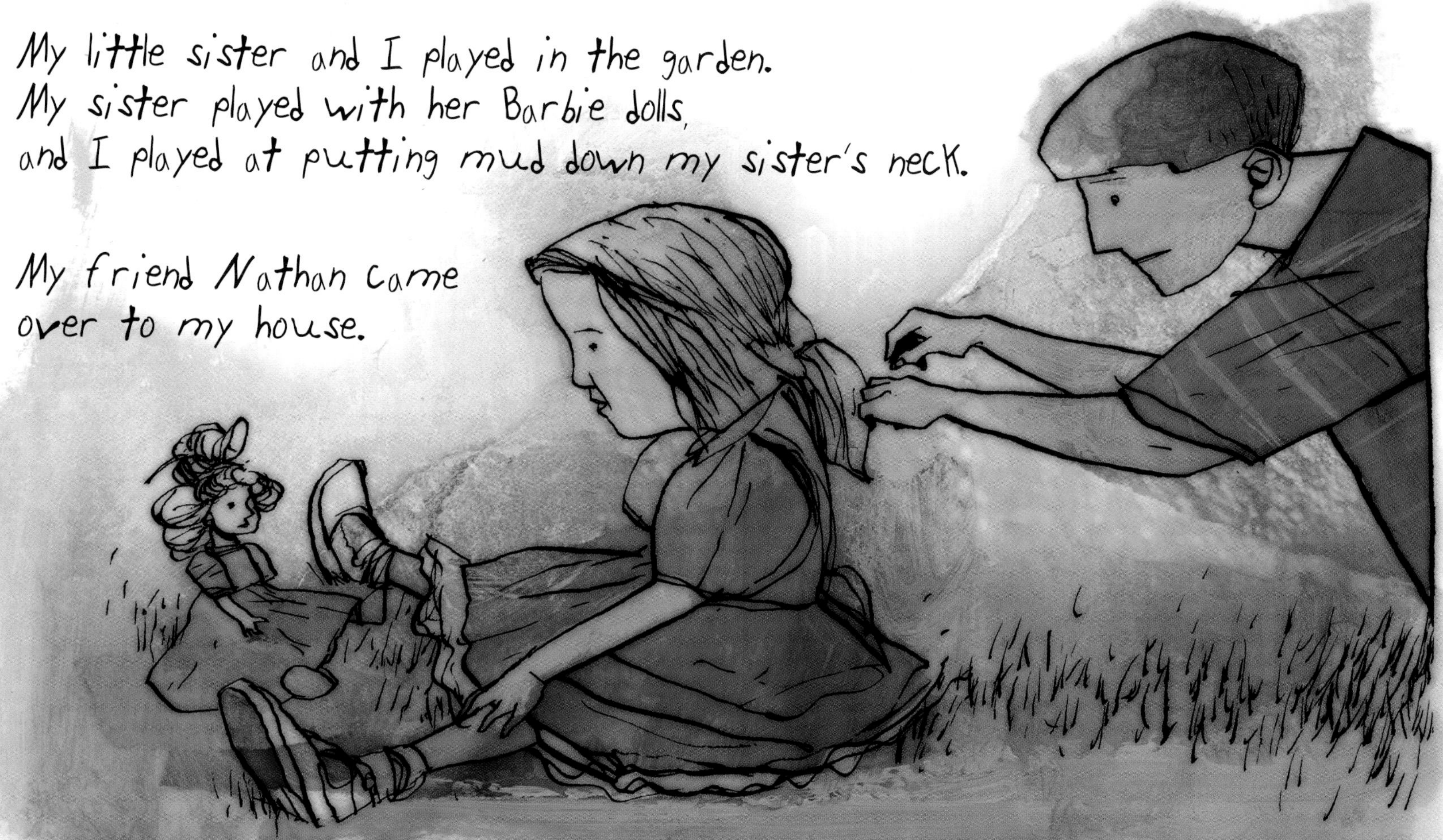
My little sister and I played in the garden.
My sister played with her Barbie dolls,
and I played at putting mud down my sister's neck.
My friend Nathan came over to my house.

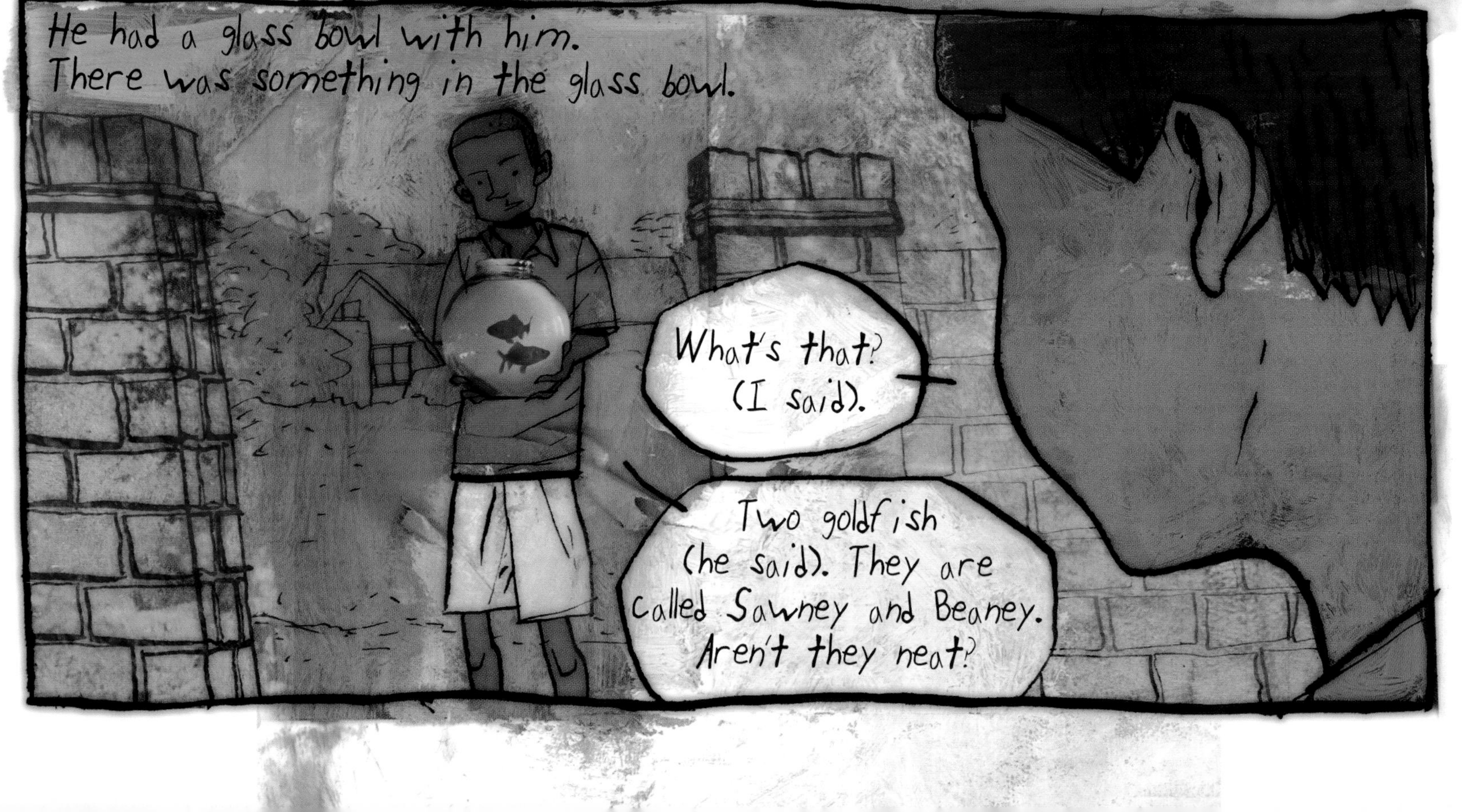
He had a glass bowl with him.
There was something in the glass bowl.
What's that? (I said).
Two goldfish (he said). They are called Sawney and Beaney. Aren't they neat?

They were pretty neat.

"I'll swap you them," I said.

"What for?" asked Nathan.

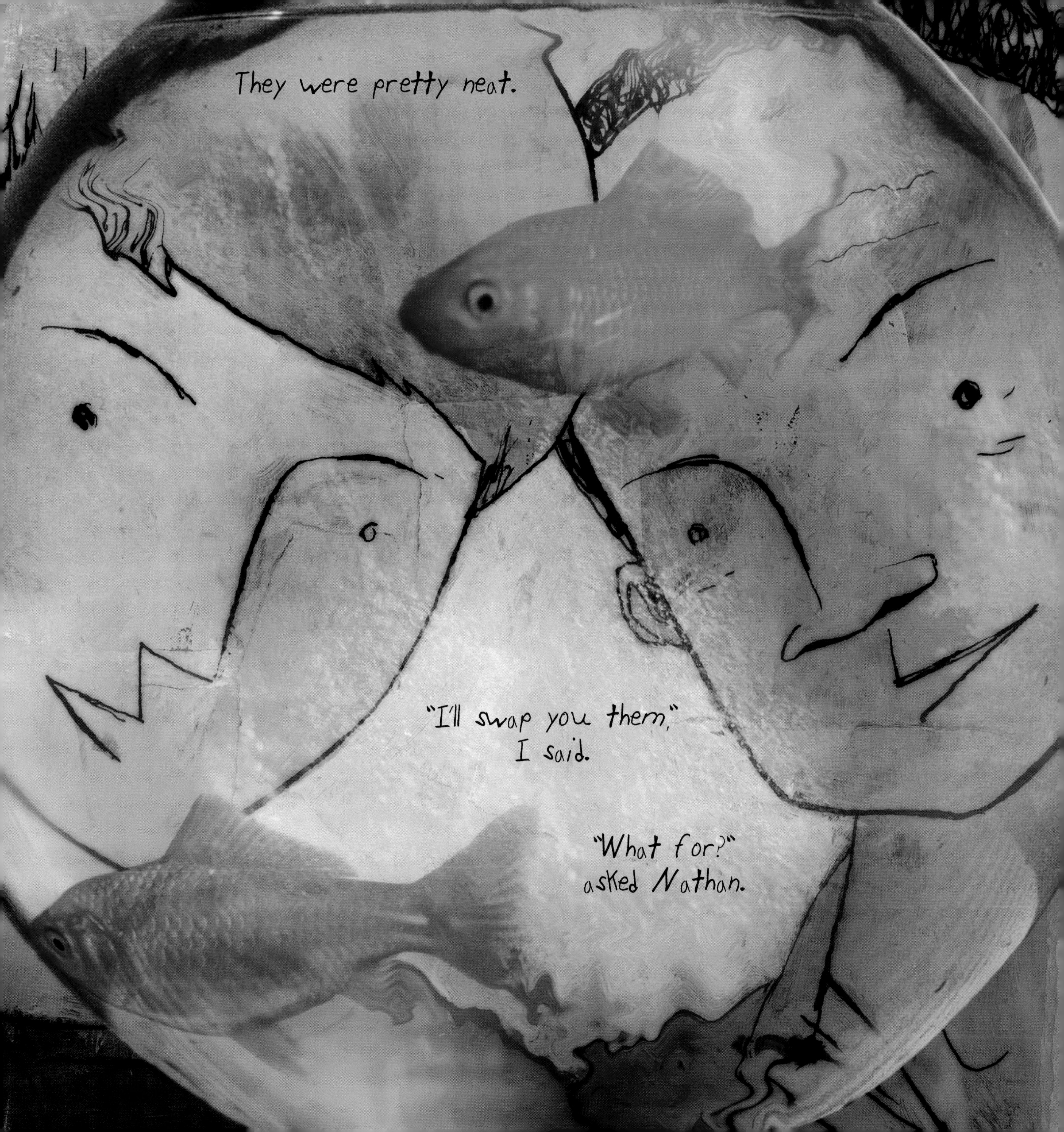

We went up to my bedroom. My little sister tagged along. I showed Nathan my old transformer robots, and my baseball cards, and my books. I showed him my old punching bag and my penny whistle that Mommy said made her head ache when I blew it. I showed him my old spaceship that didn't float in the bath anymore, and the puppet with the tangled strings, and I even showed him Clownie, my clown that I sleep with.

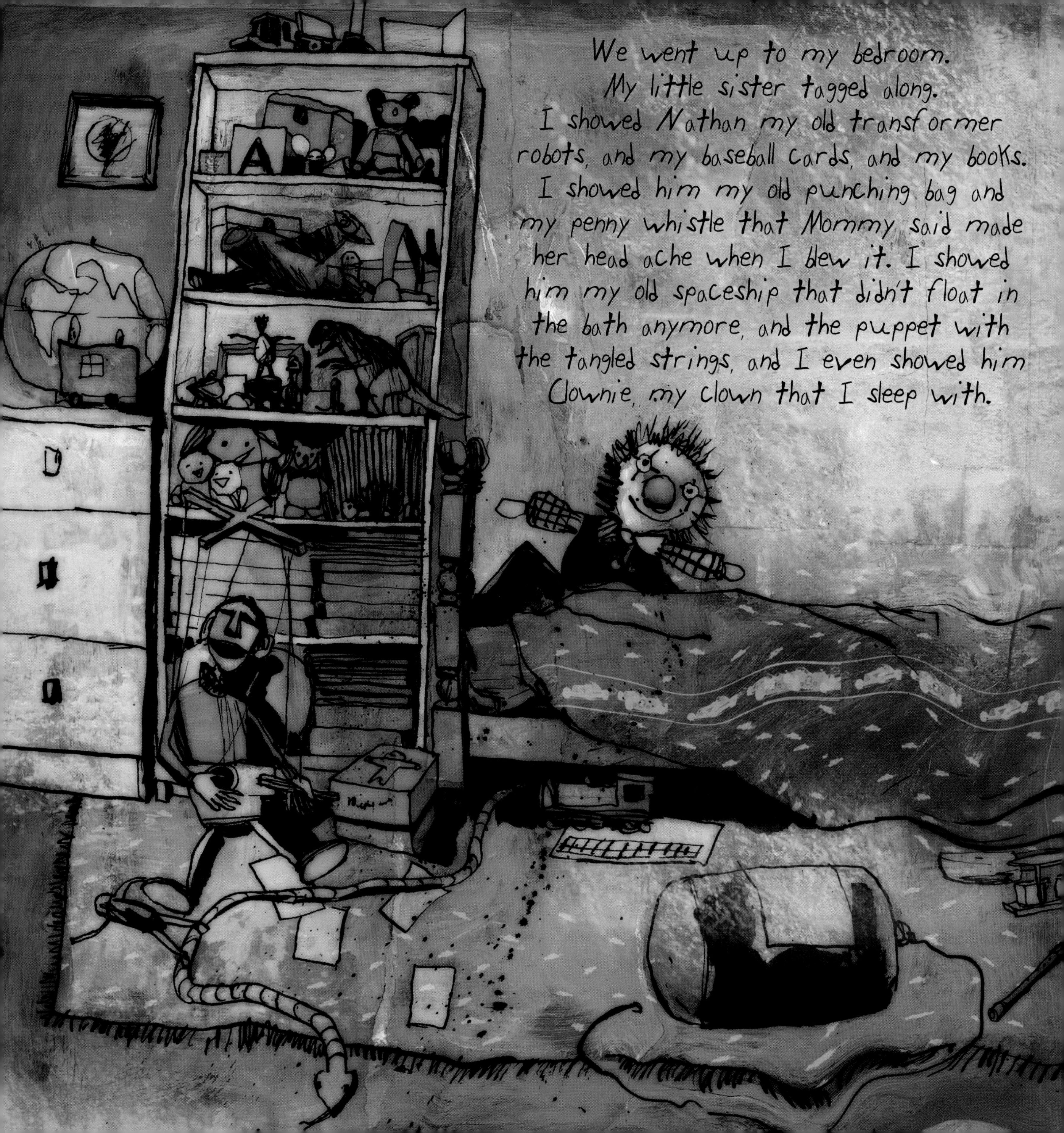

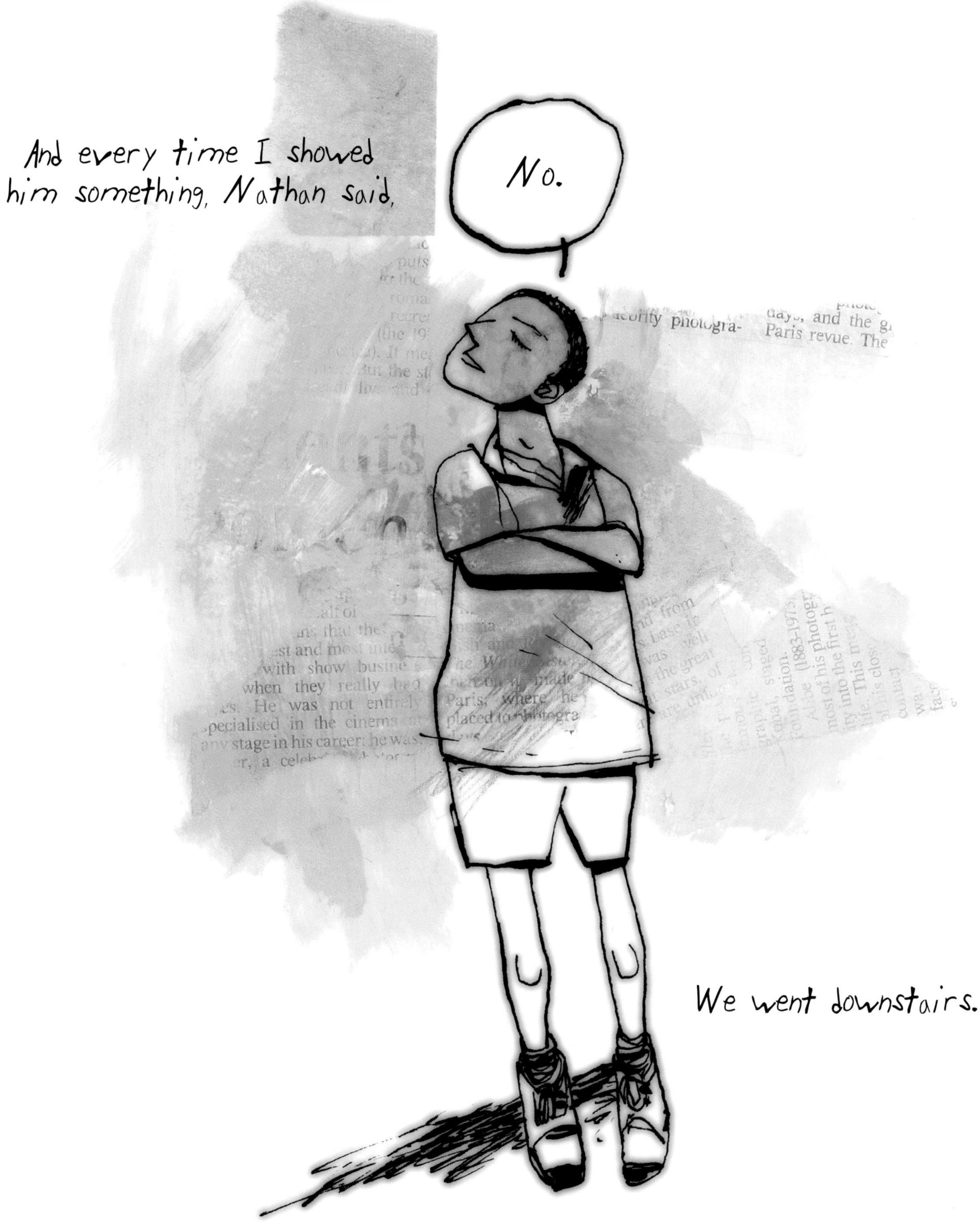
And every time I showed him something, Nathan said,
No.
We went downstairs.

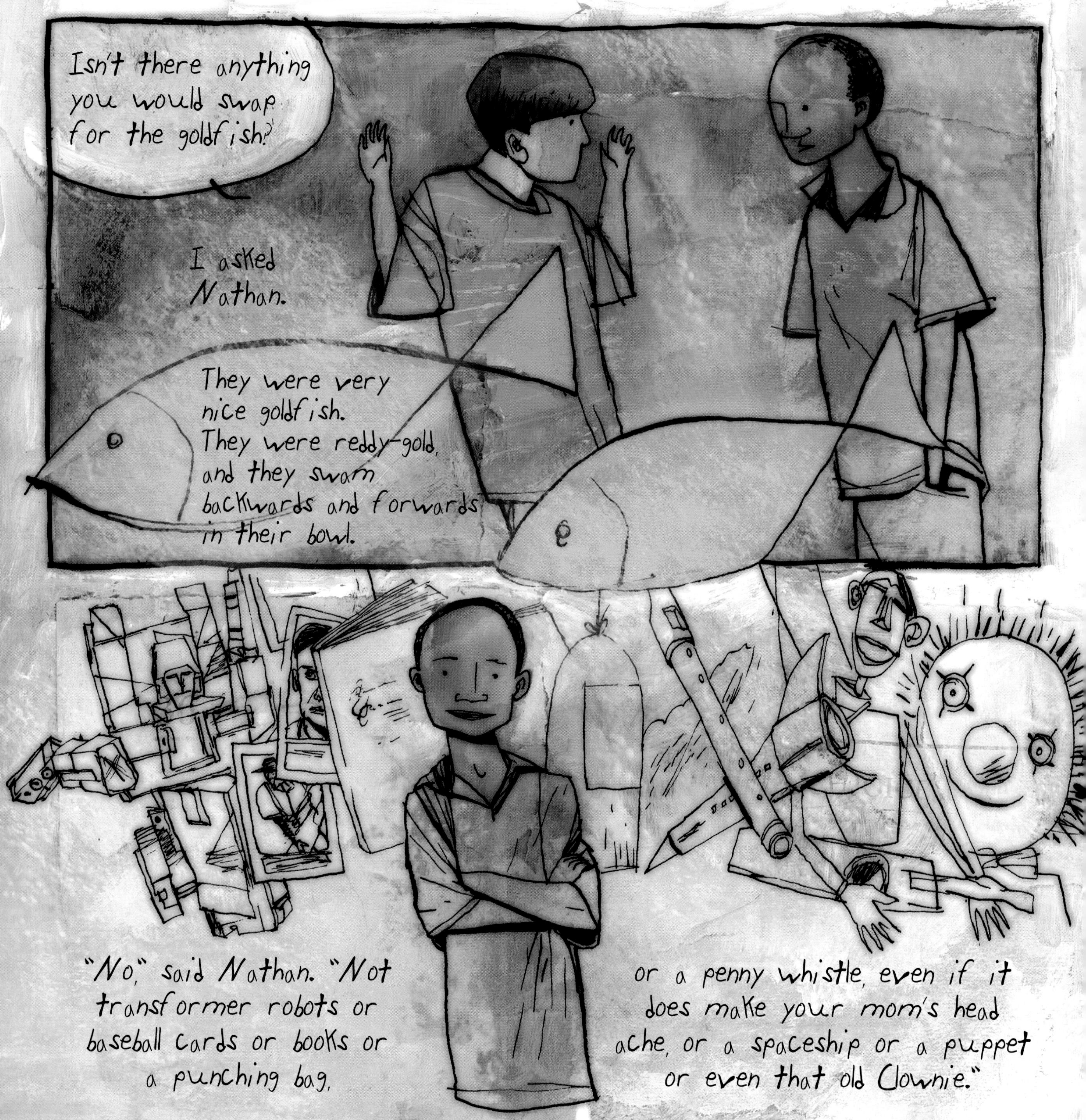
Isn't there anything you would swap for the goldfish?
I asked Nathan.
They were very nice goldfish. They were reddy-gold, and they swam backwards and forwards in their bowl.
"No," said Nathan. "Not transformer robots or baseball cards or books or a punching bag,
or a penny whistle, even if it does make your mom's head ache, or a spaceship or a puppet or even that old Clownie."

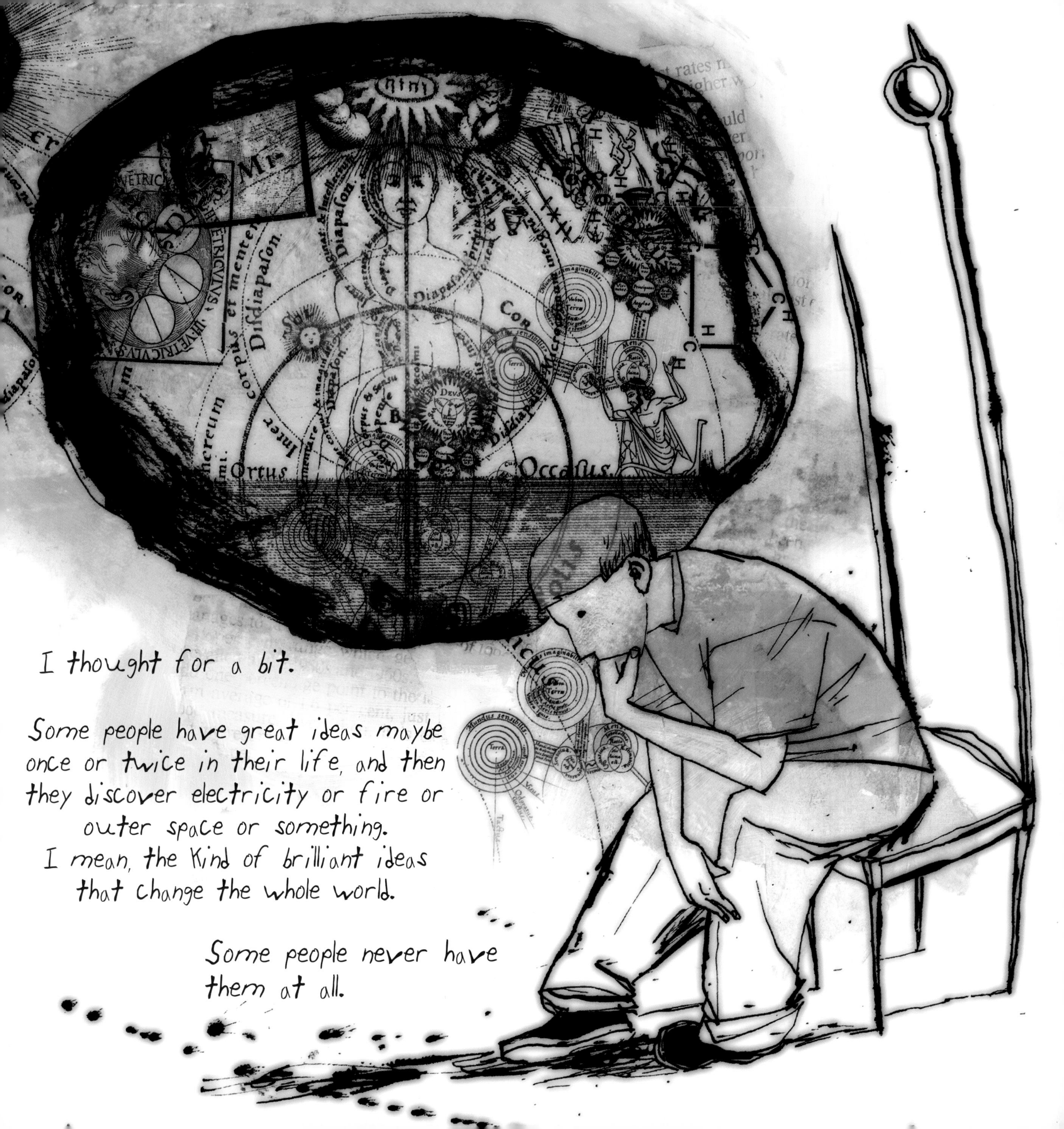
I thought for a bit.
Some people have great ideas maybe once or twice in their life, and then they discover electricity or fire or outer space or something. I mean, the Kind of brilliant ideas that change the whole world.
Some people never have them at all.

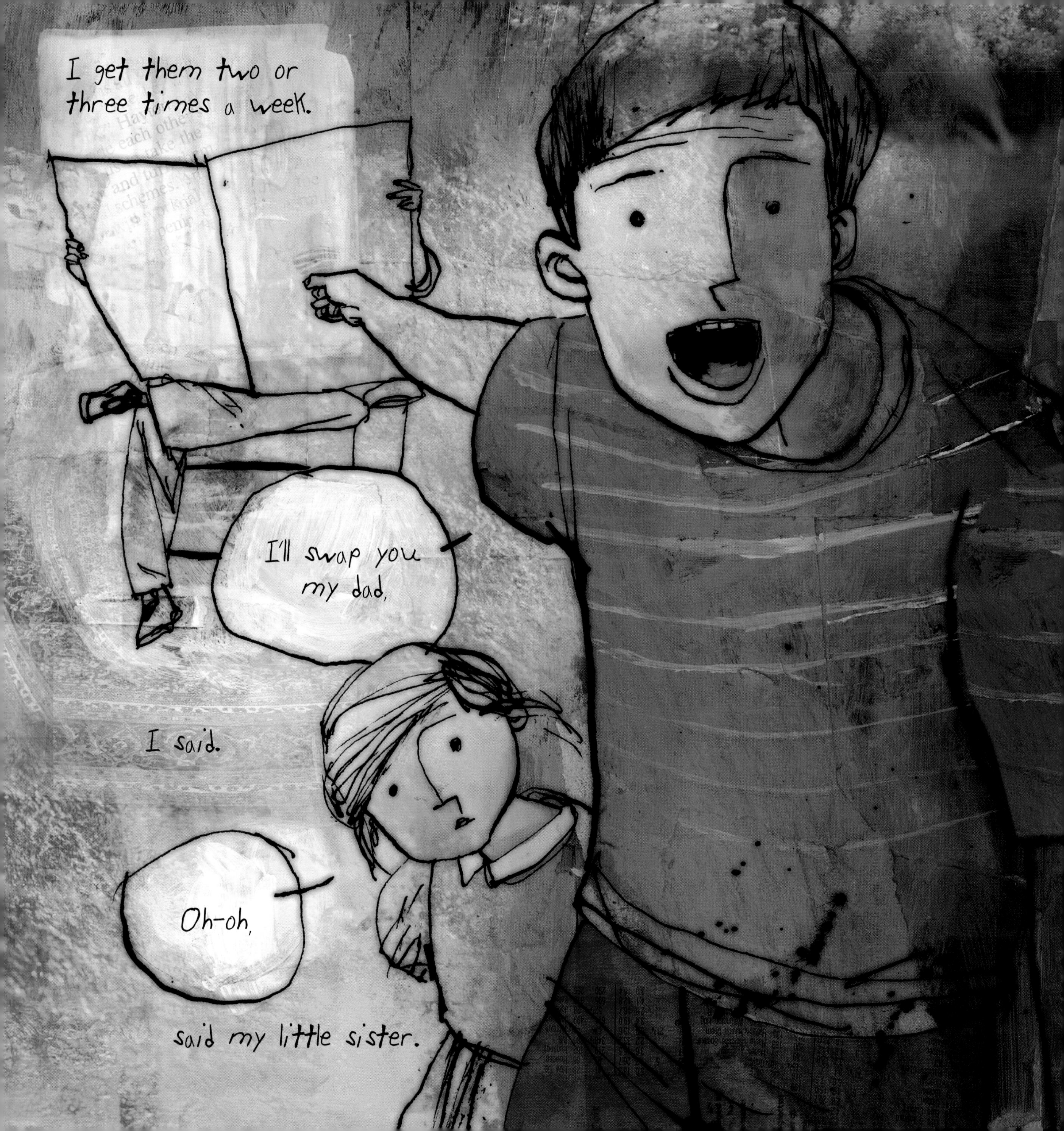
I get them two or three times a week.
I'll swap you my dad,
I said.
Oh-oh,
said my little sister.

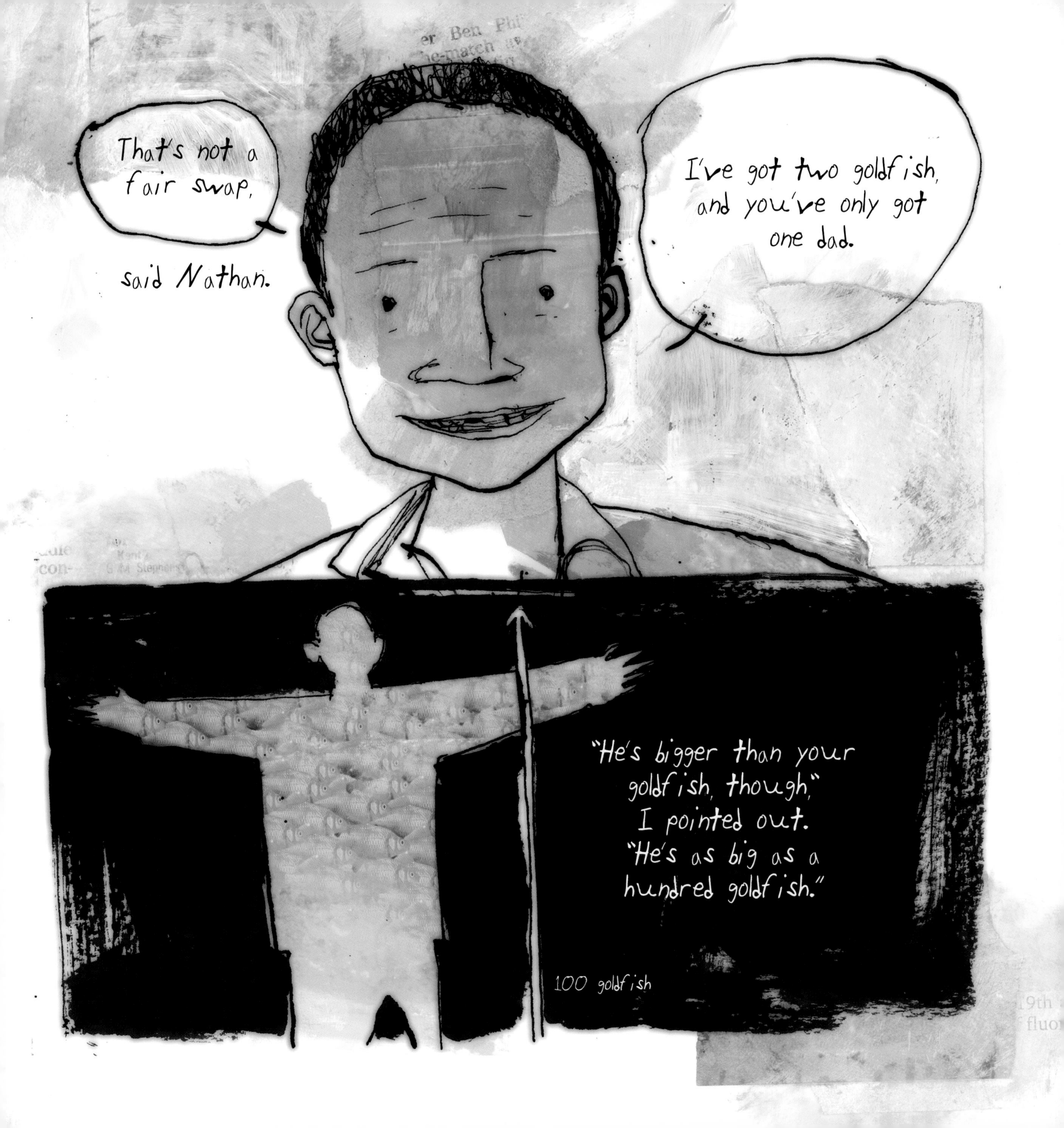
That's not a fair swap,
said Nathan.
I've got two goldfish, and you've only got one dad.
"He's bigger than your goldfish, though," I pointed out. "He's as big as a hundred goldfish."
100 goldfish

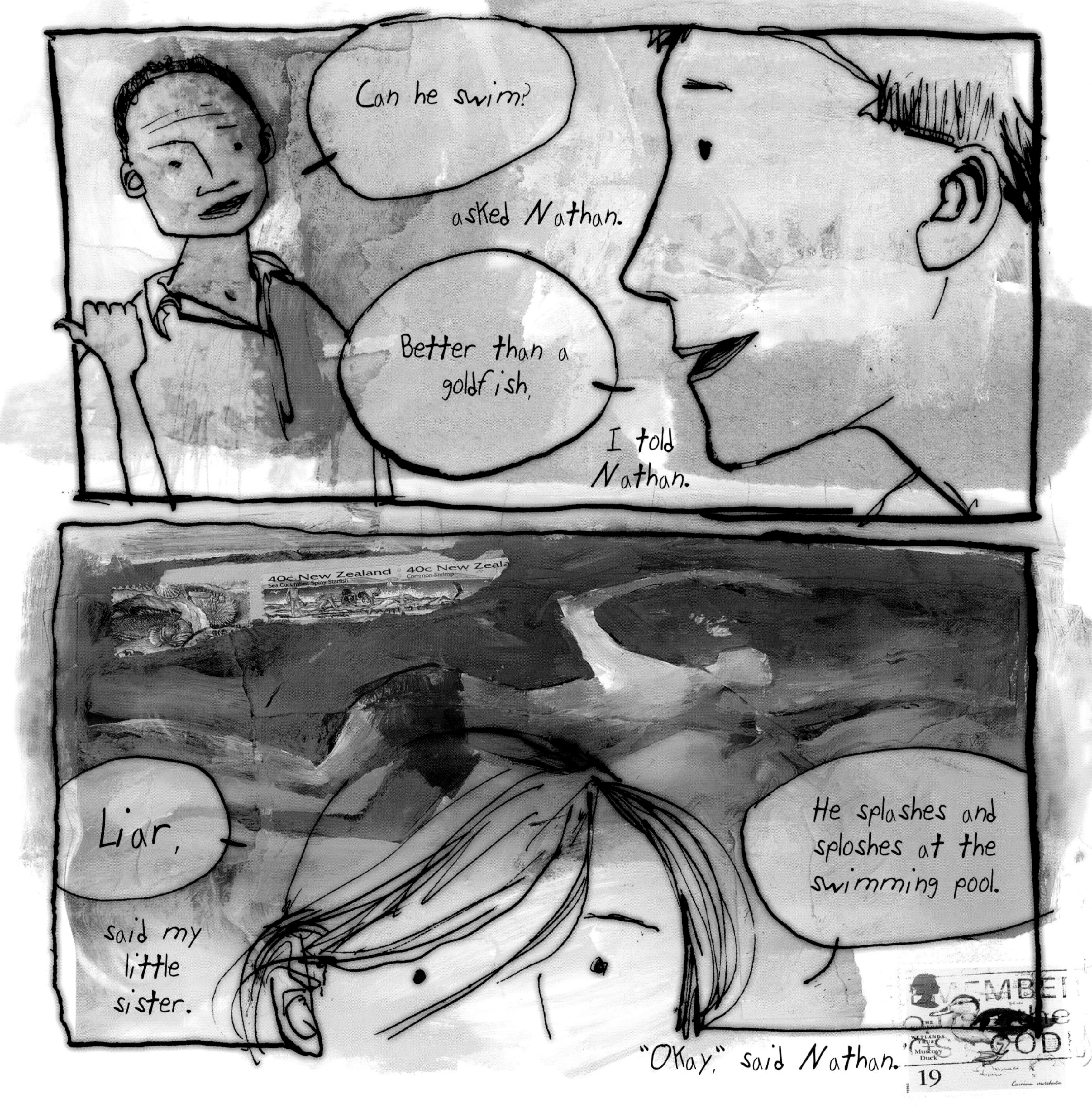
Can he swim?
asked Nathan.
Better than a goldfish,
I told Nathan.
40c New Zealand
Liar,
said my little sister.
He splashes and sploshes at the swimming pool.
"Okay," said Nathan.

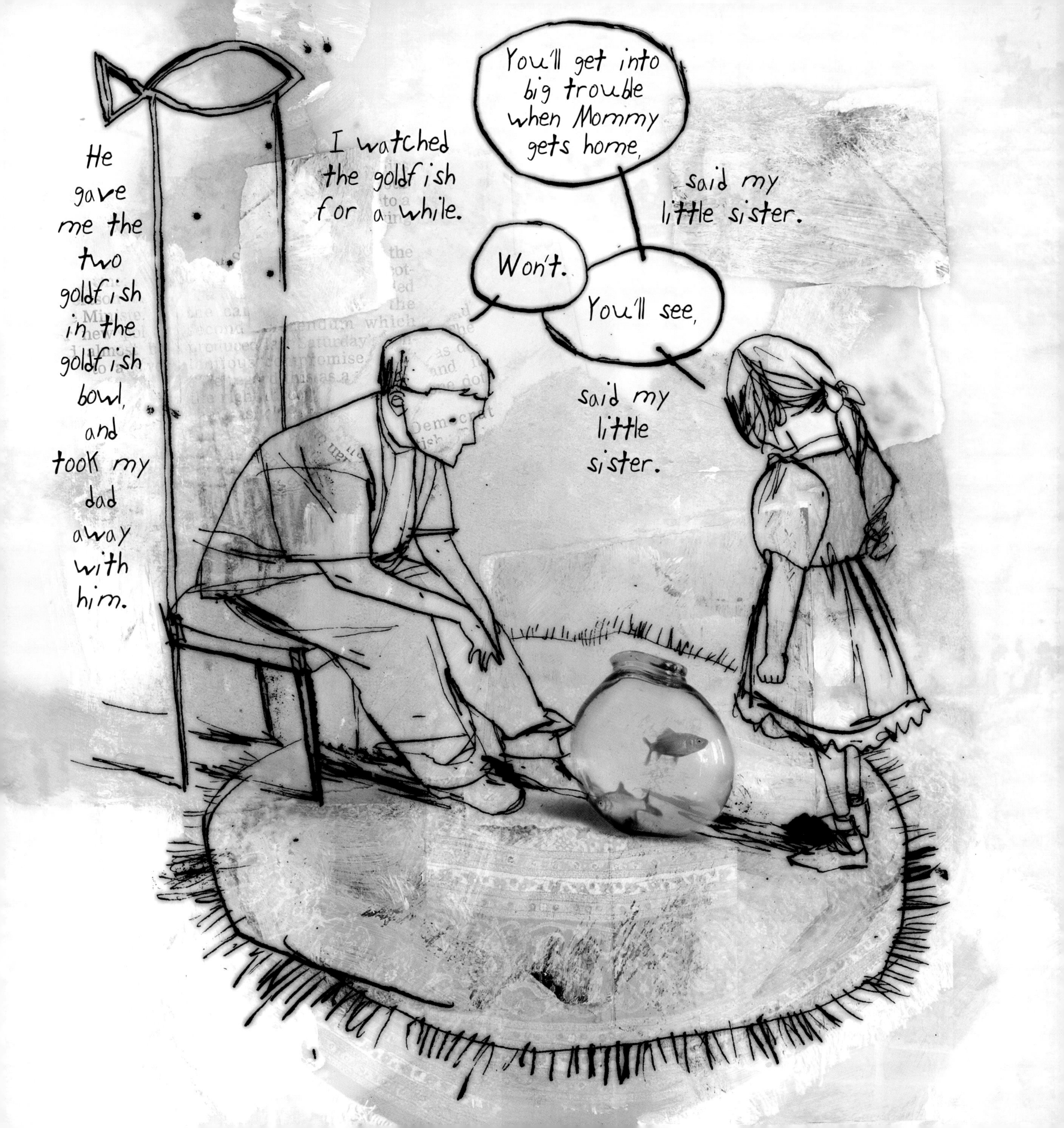
He gave me the two goldfish in the goldfish bowl, and took my dad away with him.
I watched the goldfish for a while.
You'll get into big trouble when Mommy gets home,
said my little sister.
Won't.
You'll see,
said my little sister.

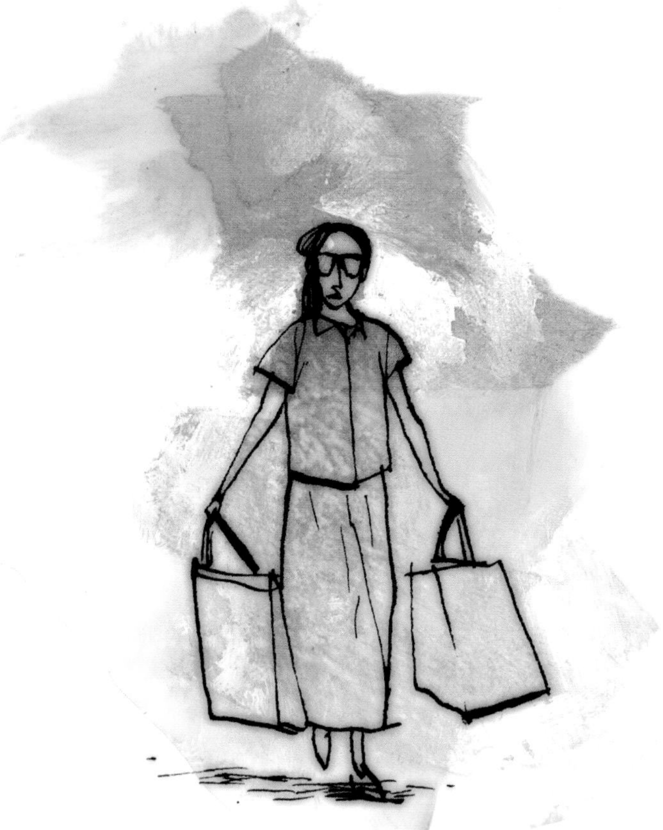

When my mother came home I said, "Mom, can we buy some goldfish food?"

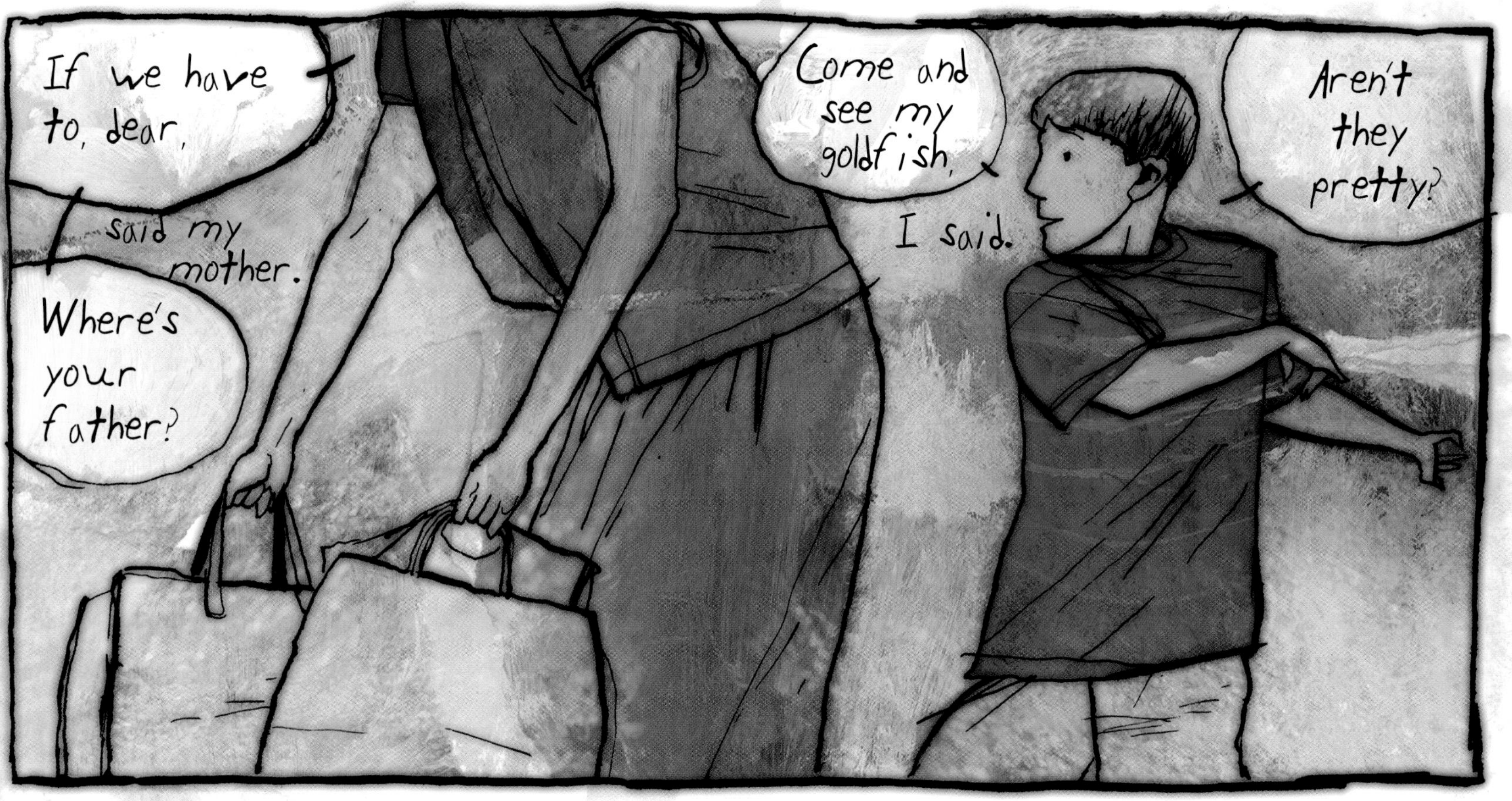
If we have to, dear,
said my mother.
Where's your father?
Come and see my goldfish,
I said.
Aren't they pretty?

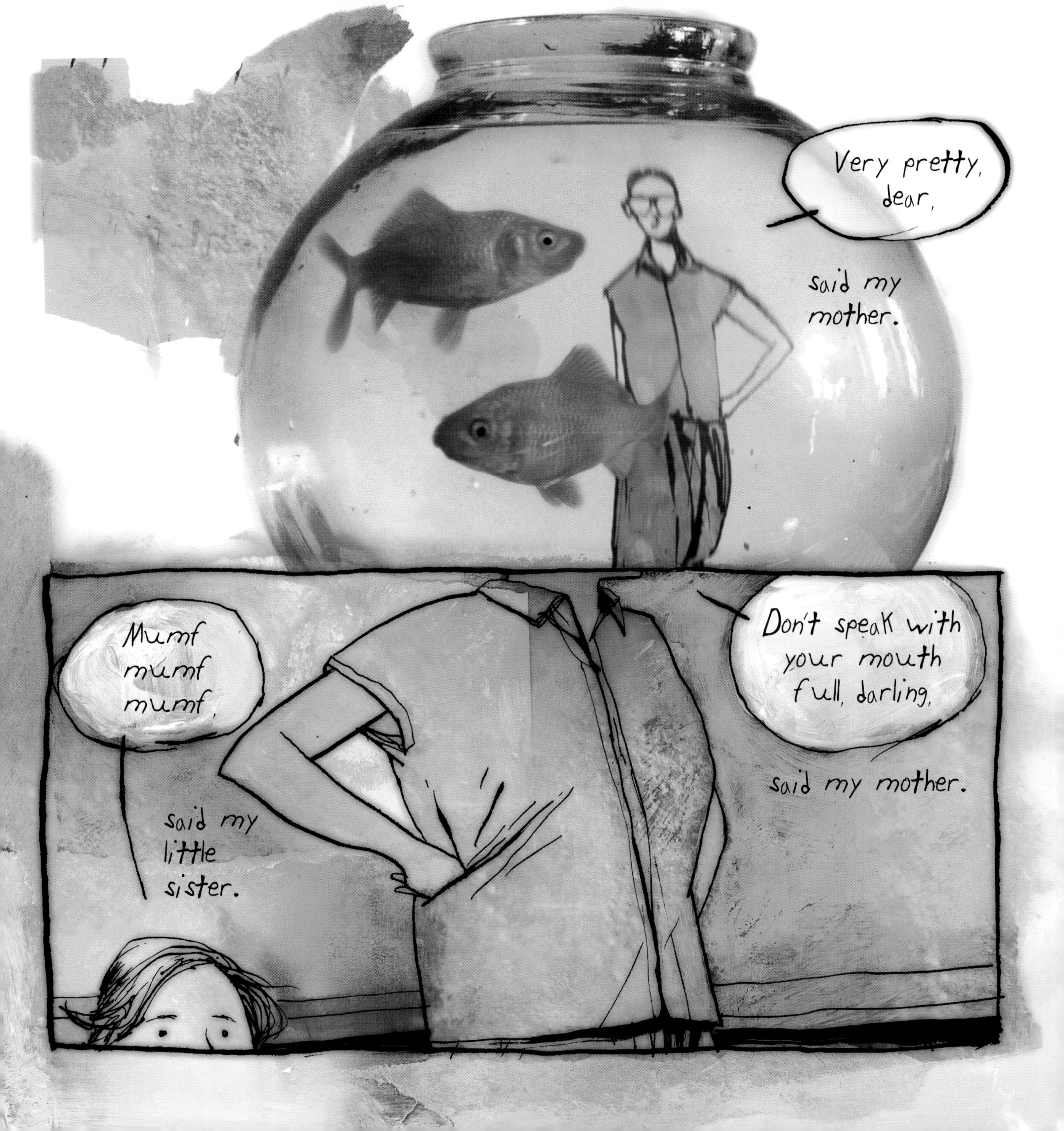
Very pretty, dear,
said my mother.
Mumf mumf mumf,
said my little sister.
Don't speak with your mouth full, darling,
said my mother.

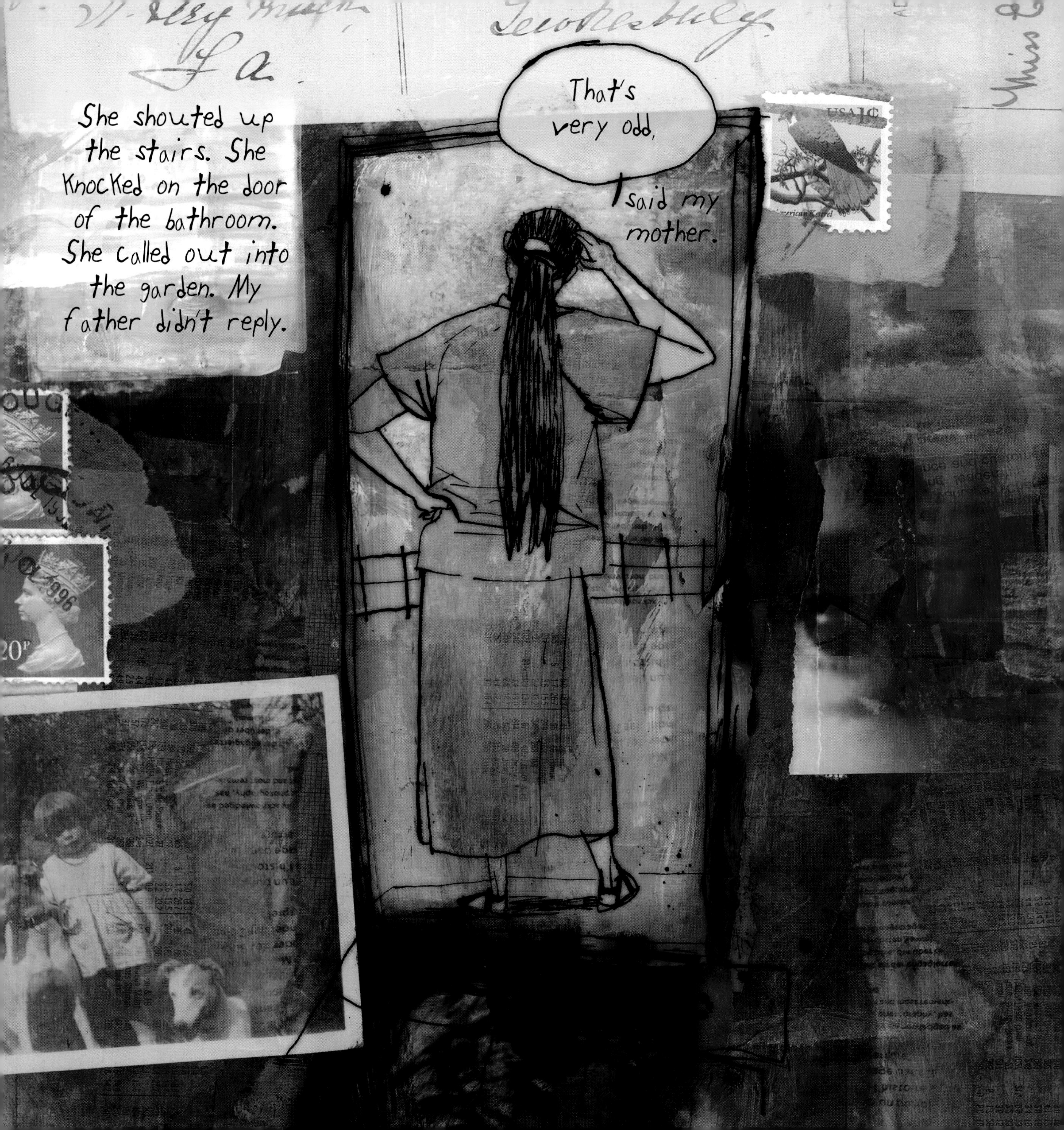
She shouted up the stairs. She knocked on the door of the bathroom. She called out into the garden. My father didn't reply.
That's very odd,
said my mother.

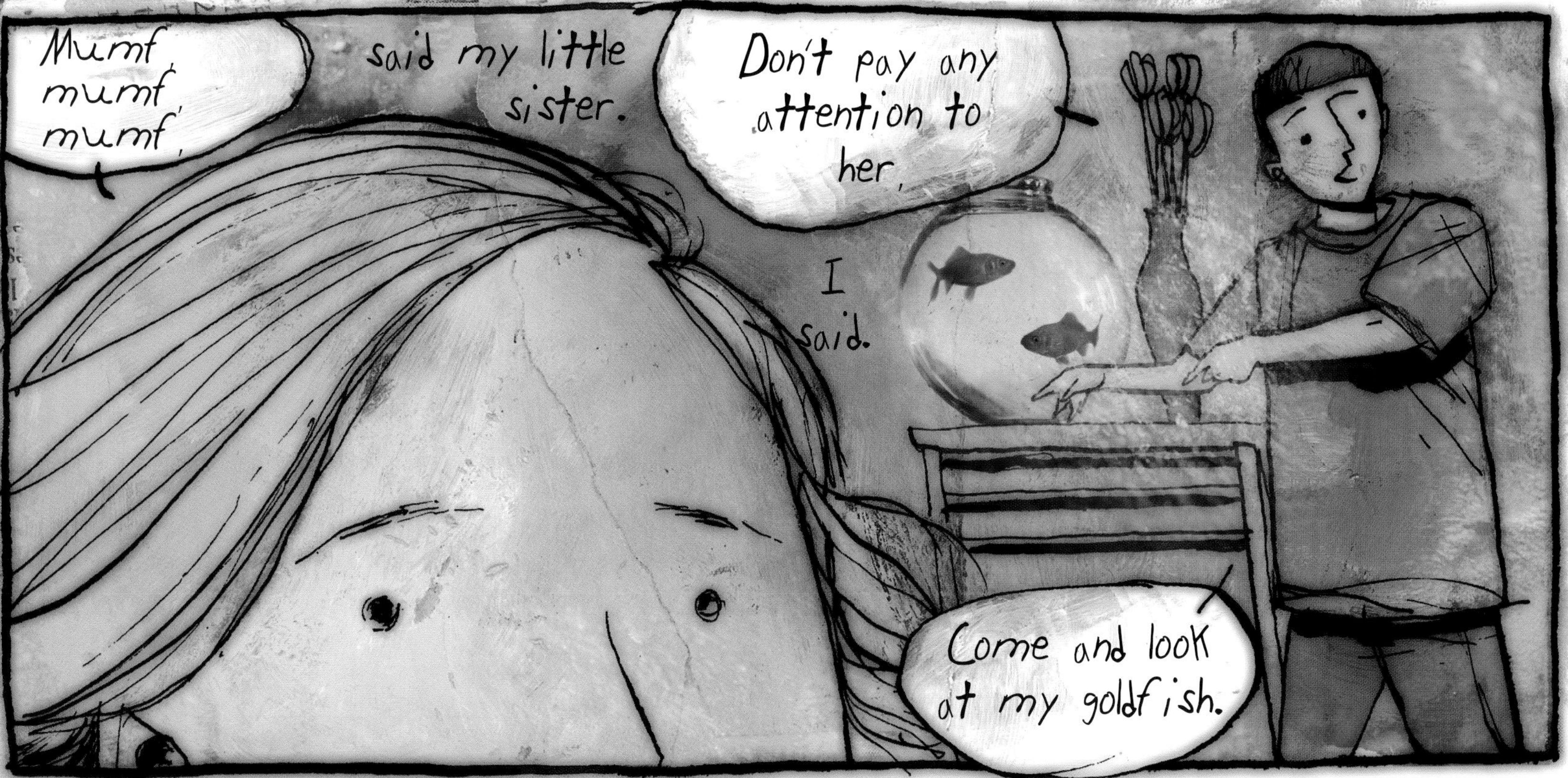
Mumf, mumf, mumf,
said my little sister.
Don't pay any attention to her,
I said.
Come and look at my goldfish.

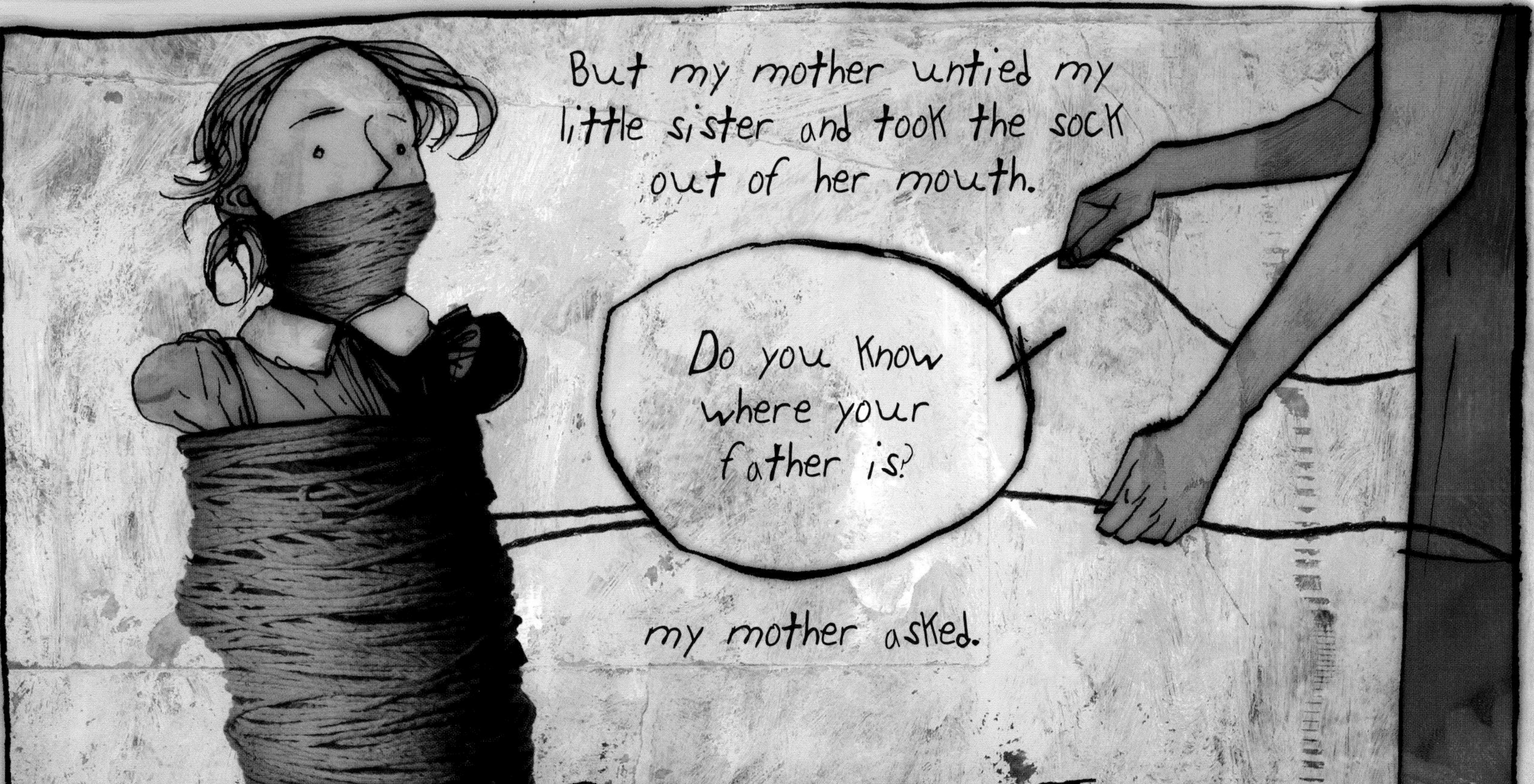
But my mother untied my little sister and took the sock out of her mouth.
Do you know where your father is?
my mother asked.

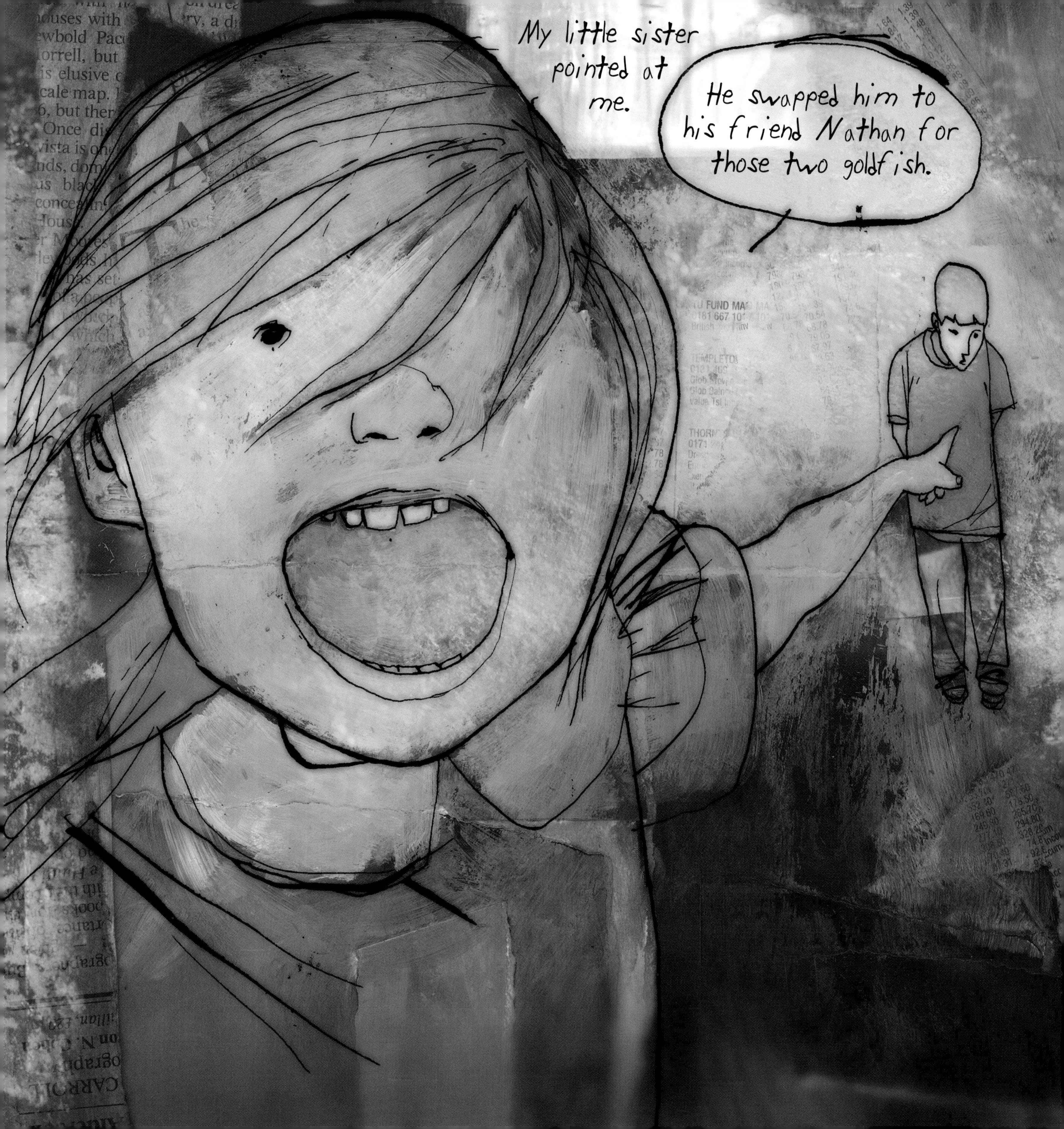
My little sister pointed at me.
He swapped him to his friend Nathan for those two goldfish.

My mother looked at me sharply.

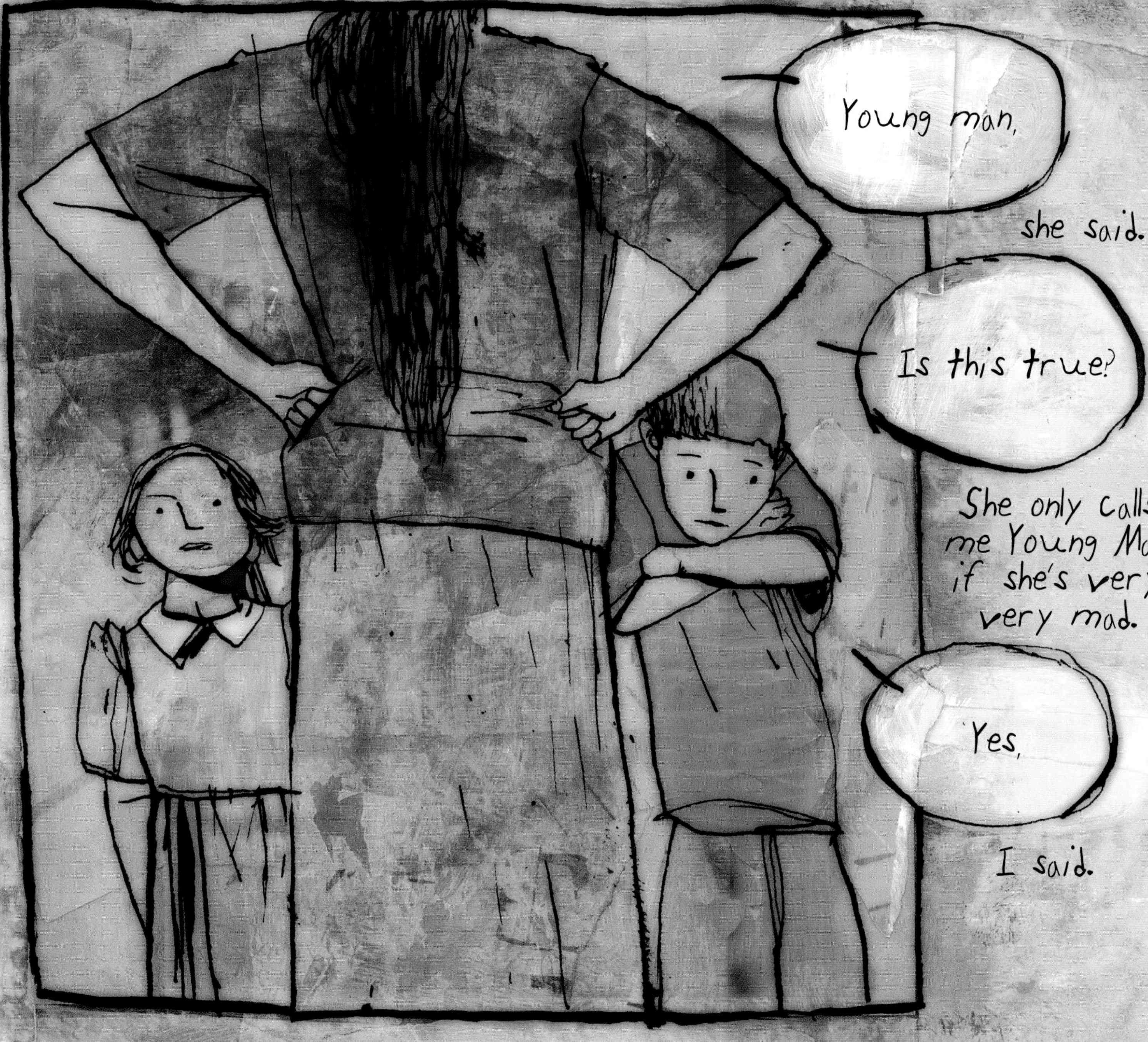
Young man,
Is this true?
Yes,

she said.

She only calls me Young Man if she's very, very mad.

I said.

"Right," said my mother, and she picked up the bowl of goldfish and handed it to me. "You can take these goldfish over to Nathan this minute, and don't you come back without your father."

"I told you so," said my little sister.

"And you can go with him," said my mother. "Fancy allowing your brother to swap your father for two goldfish and a bowl. The very idea."

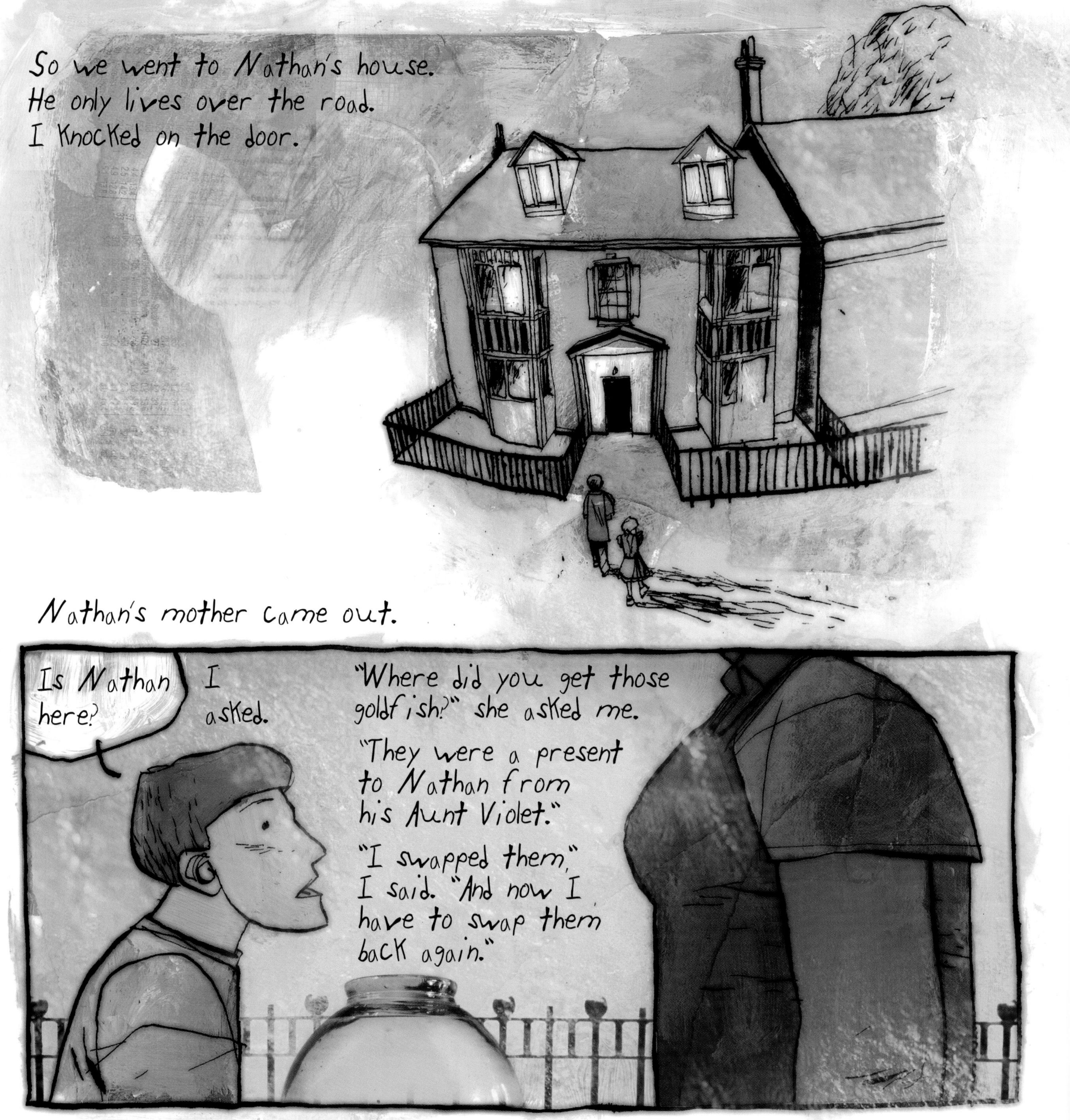
So we went to Nathan's house.
He only lives over the road.
I knocked on the door.
Nathan's mother came out.
Is Nathan here?
I asked.
"Where did you get those goldfish?" she asked me.
"They were a present to Nathan from his Aunt Violet."
"I swapped them," I said. "And now I have to swap them back again."

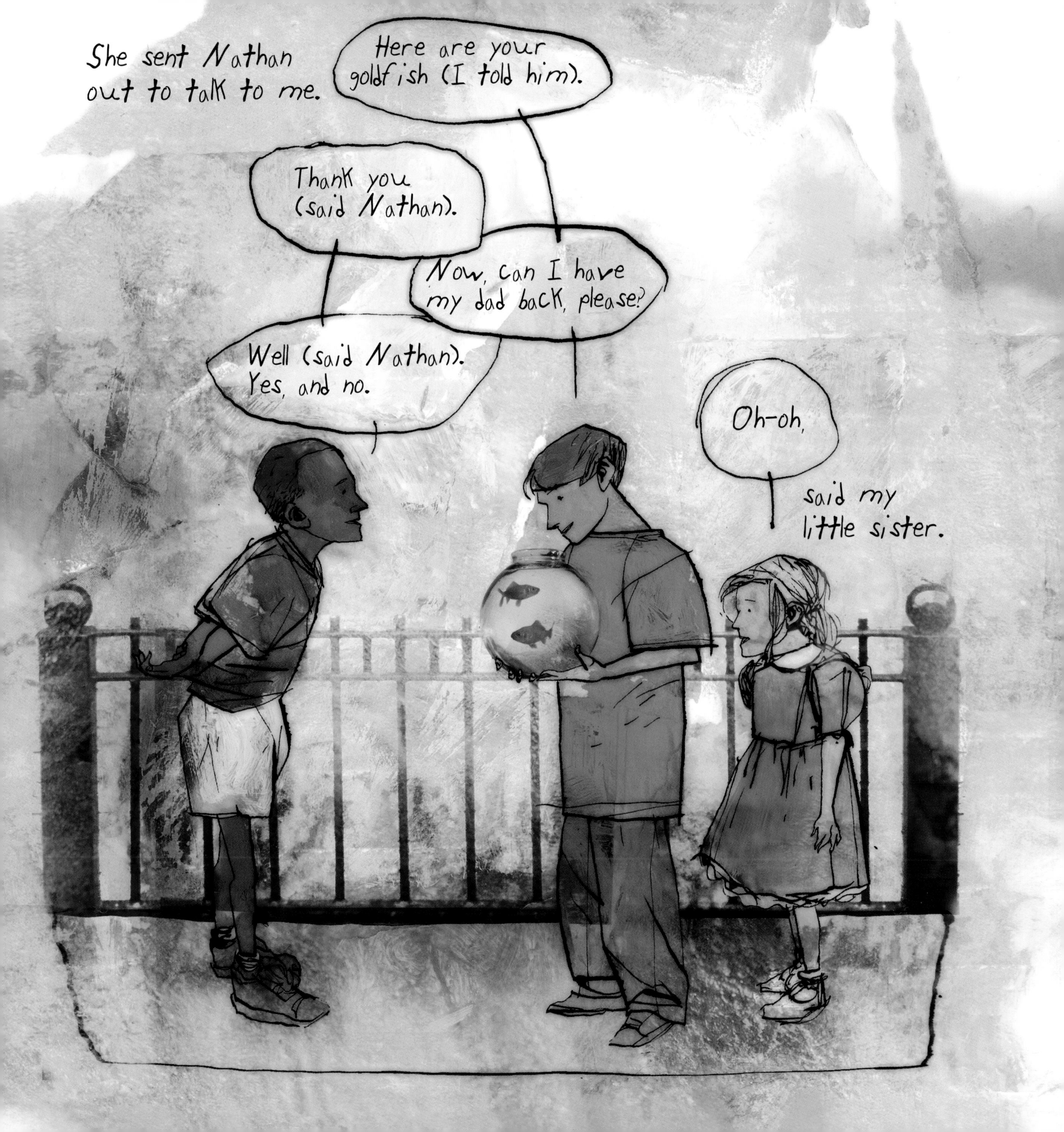
She sent Nathan out to talk to me.
Here are your goldfish (I told him).
Thank you (said Nathan).
Now, can I have my dad back, please?
Well (said Nathan). Yes, and no.
Oh-oh,
said my little sister.

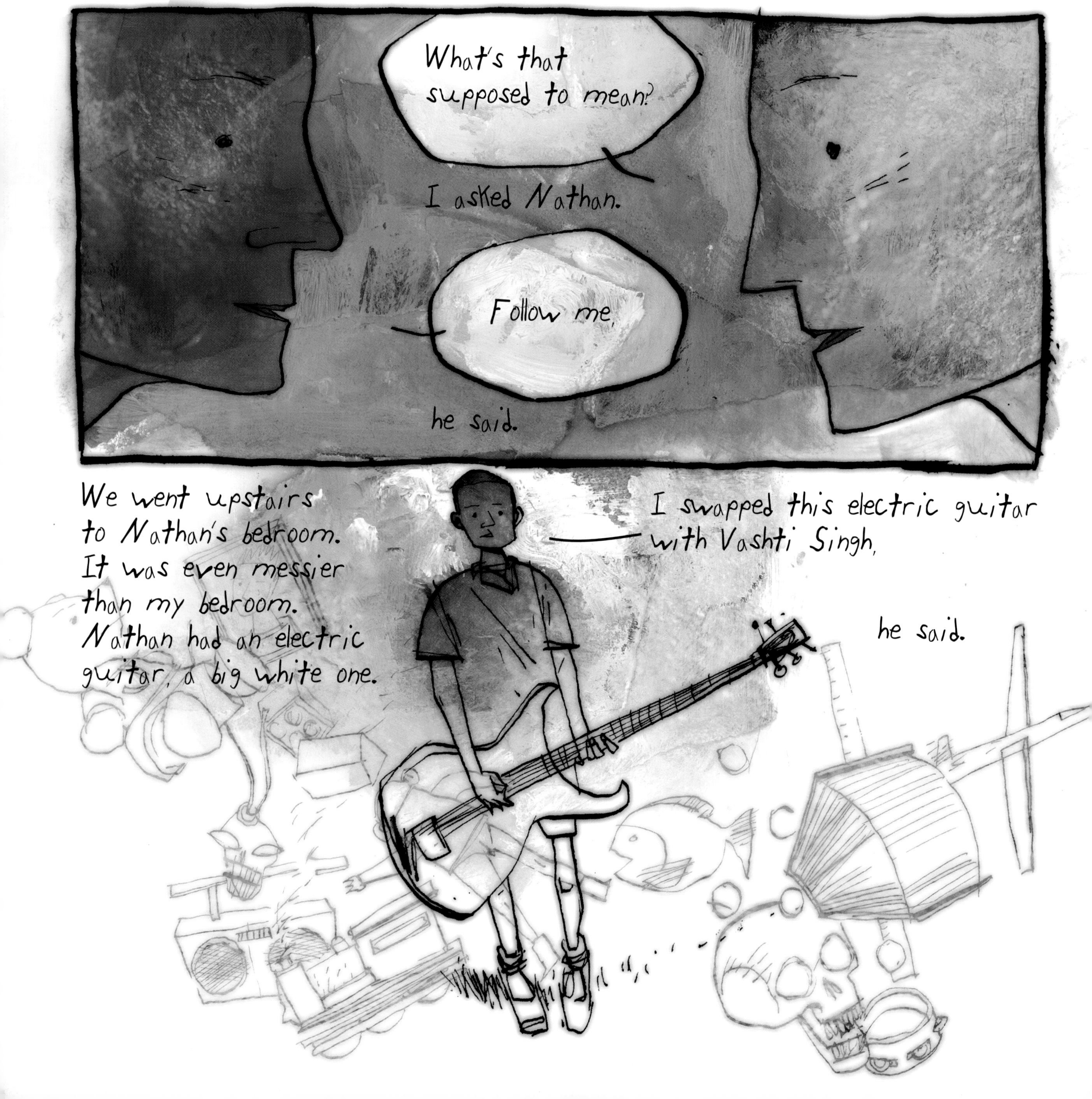
What's that supposed to mean?
I asked Nathan.
Follow me,
he said.
We went upstairs to Nathan's bedroom. It was even messier than my bedroom. Nathan had an electric guitar, a big white one.
I swapped this electric guitar with Vashti Singh,
he said.

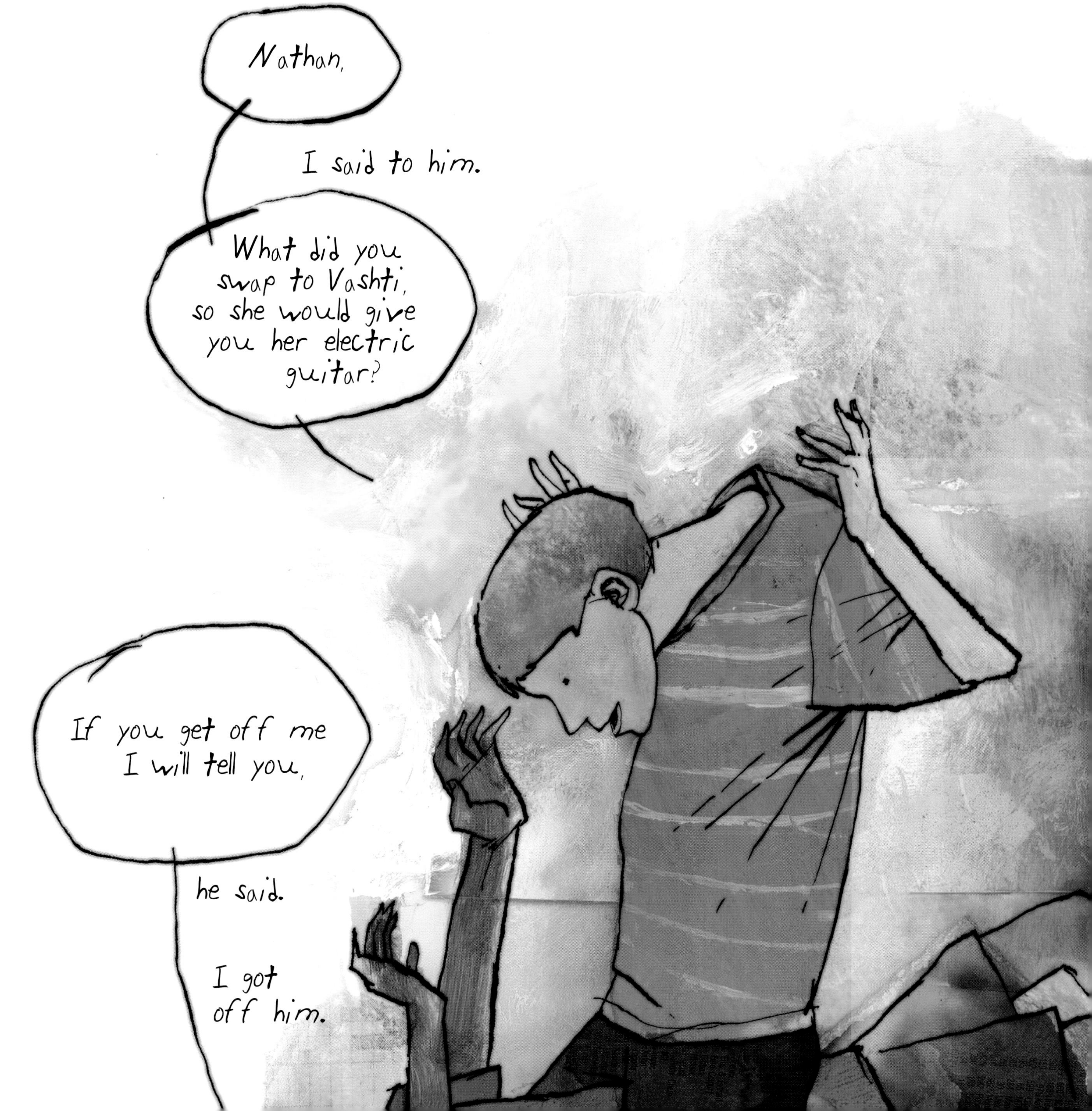
Nathan,
I said to him.
What did you swap to Vashti, so she would give you her electric guitar?
If you get off me I will tell you,
he said.
I got off him.

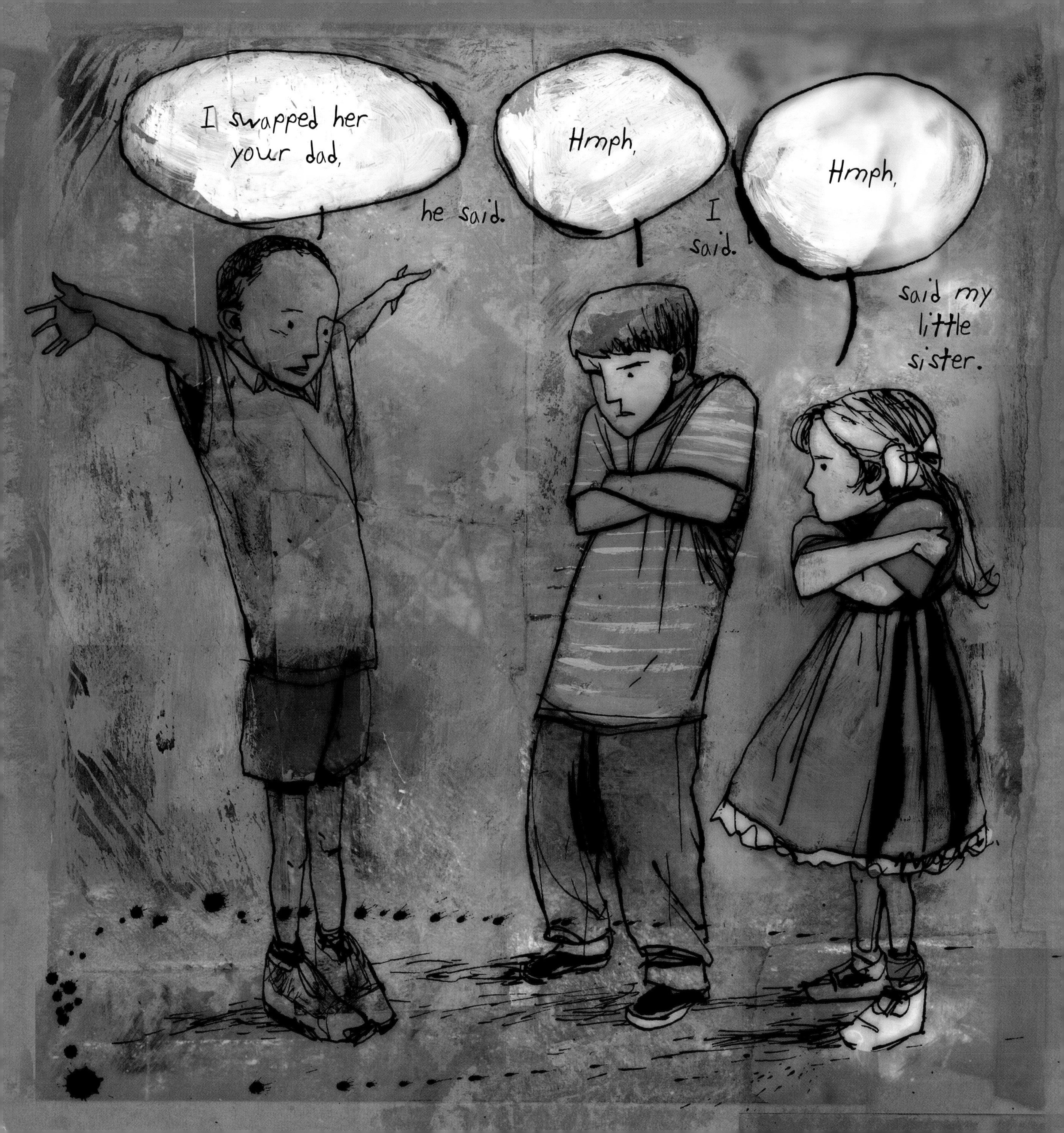

I swapped her your dad,
he said.
Hmph,
I said.
Hmph,
said my little sister.

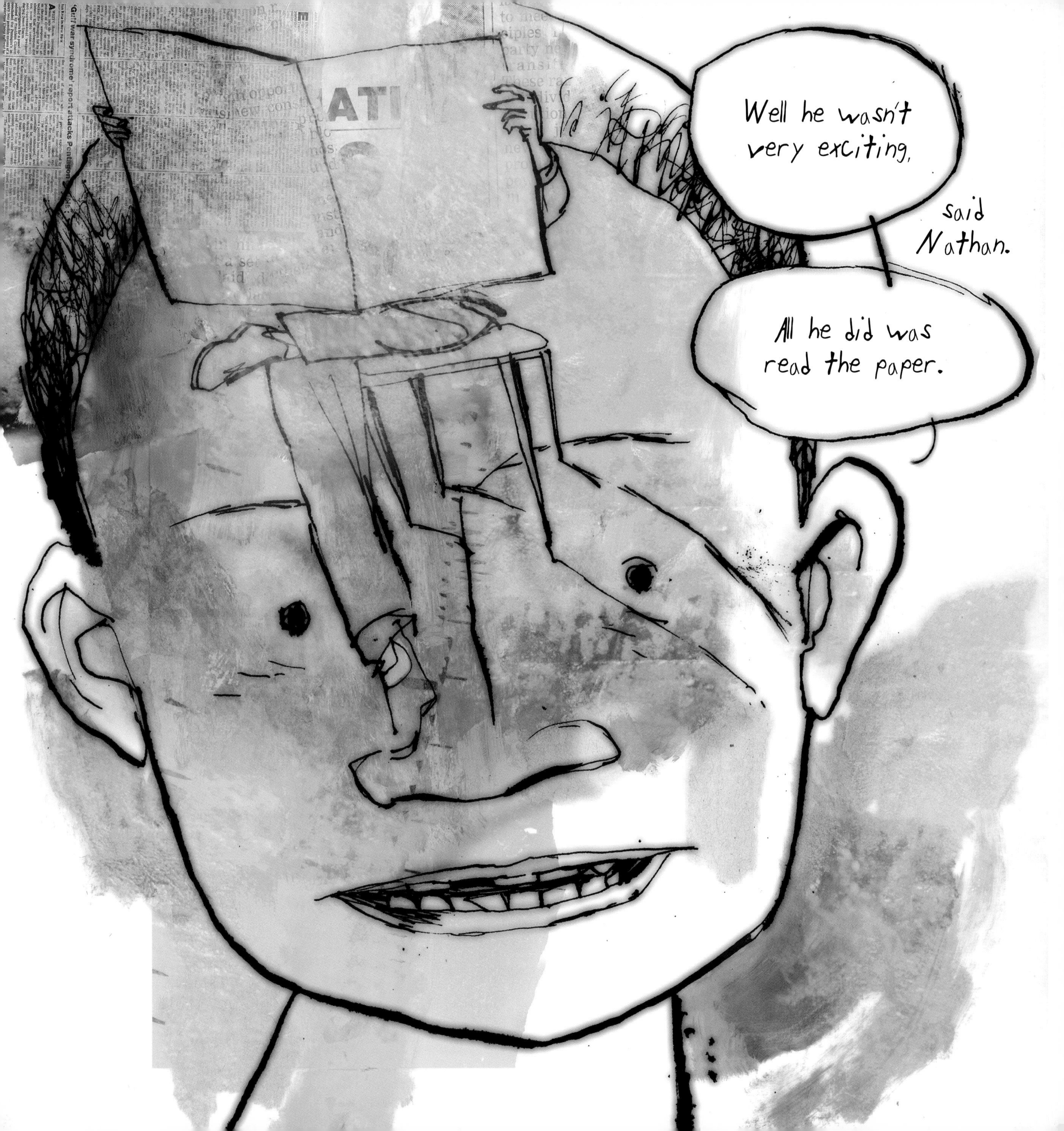
Well he wasn't very exciting,
said Nathan.
All he did was read the paper.

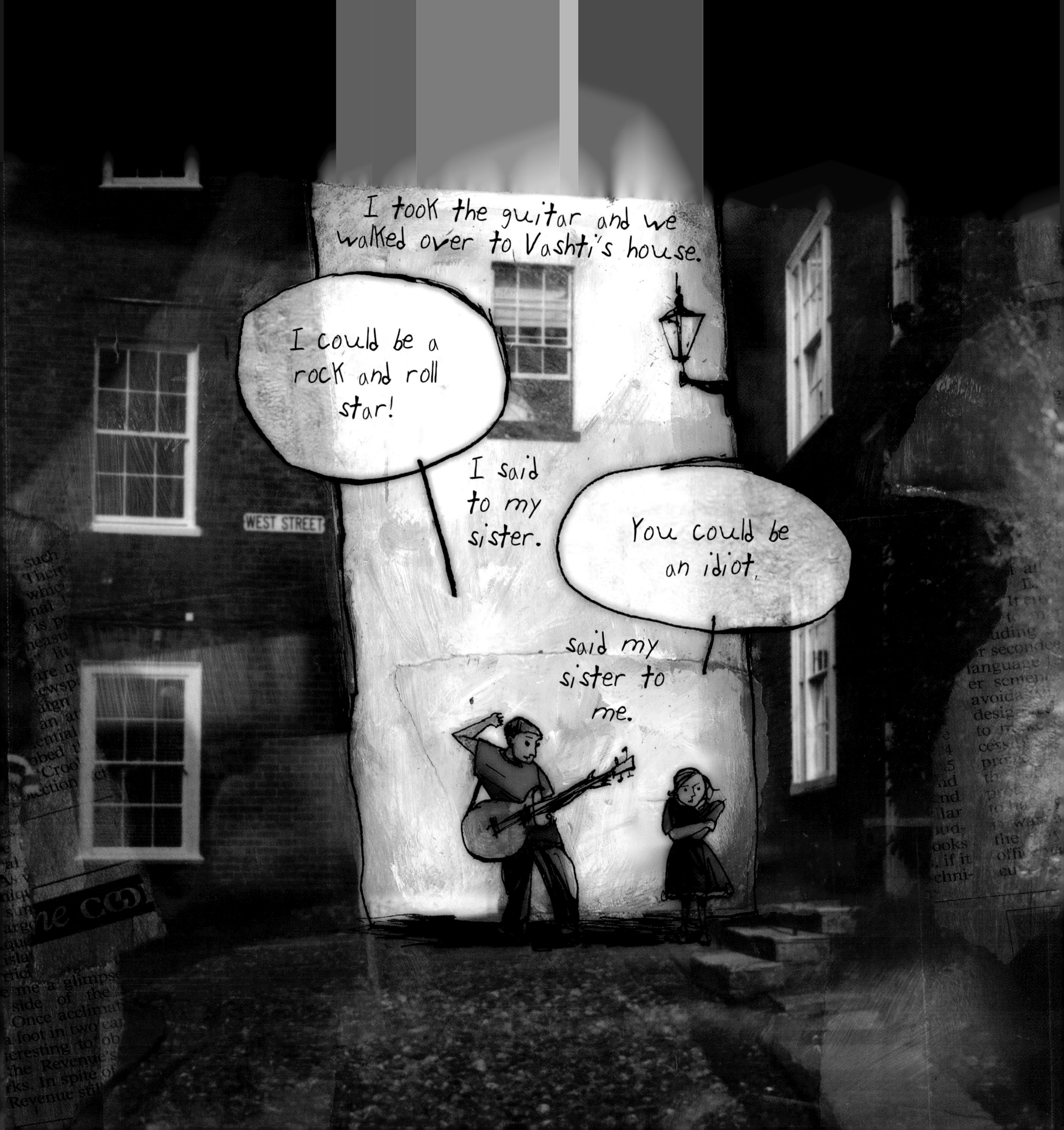
I took the guitar and we walked over to Vashti's house.
I could be a rock and roll star!
I said to my sister.
WEST STREET
You could be an idiot,
said my sister to me.

I rang Vashti's doorbell.

"I've got your guitar for you," I said to Vashti.

Vashti giggled. All Vashti's sisters giggled too.

"Can I have my dad back, please?"

They giggled again.

"Please, Vashti," said my little sister.

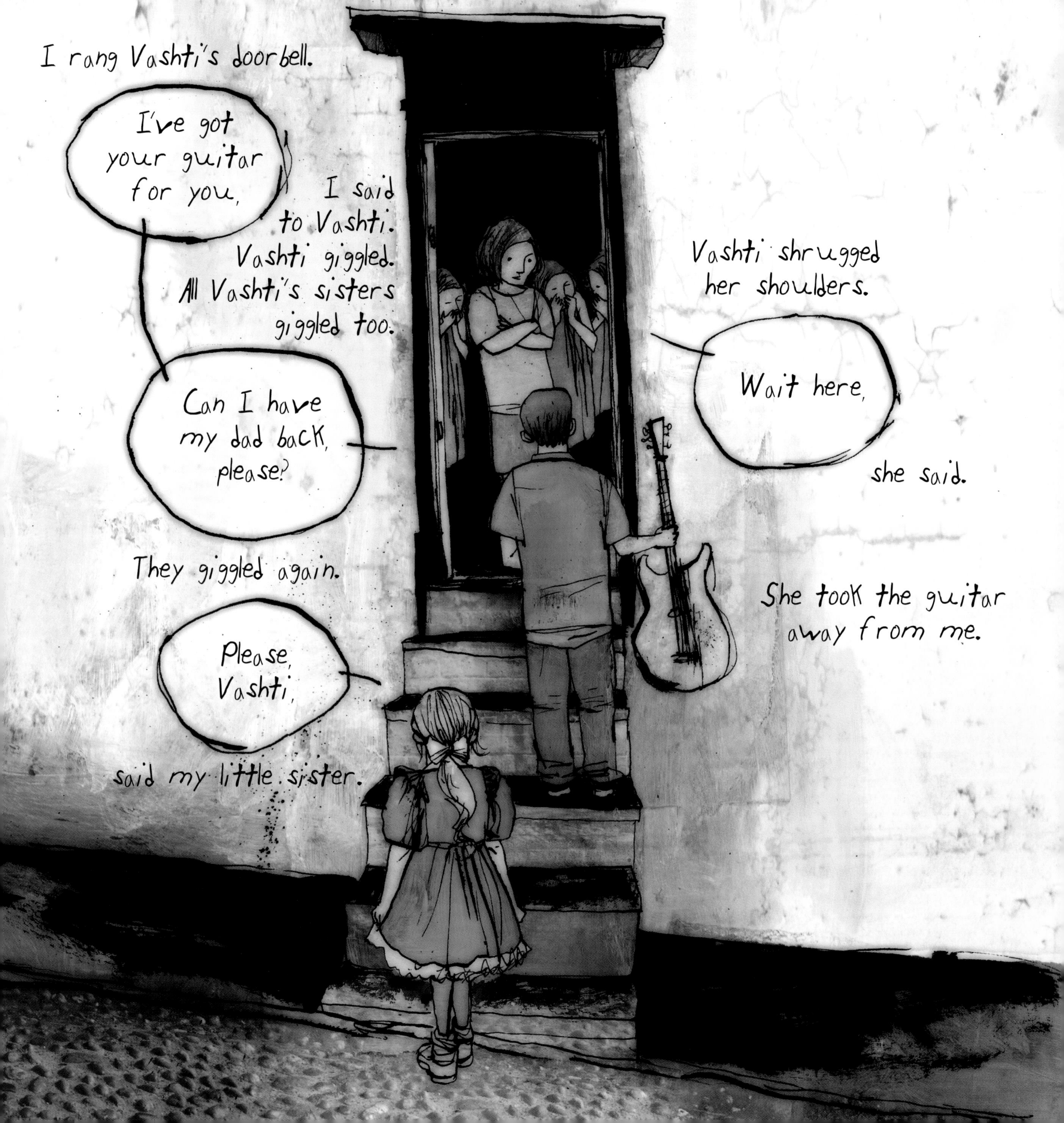

Vashti shrugged her shoulders.

"Wait here," she said.

She took the guitar away from me.

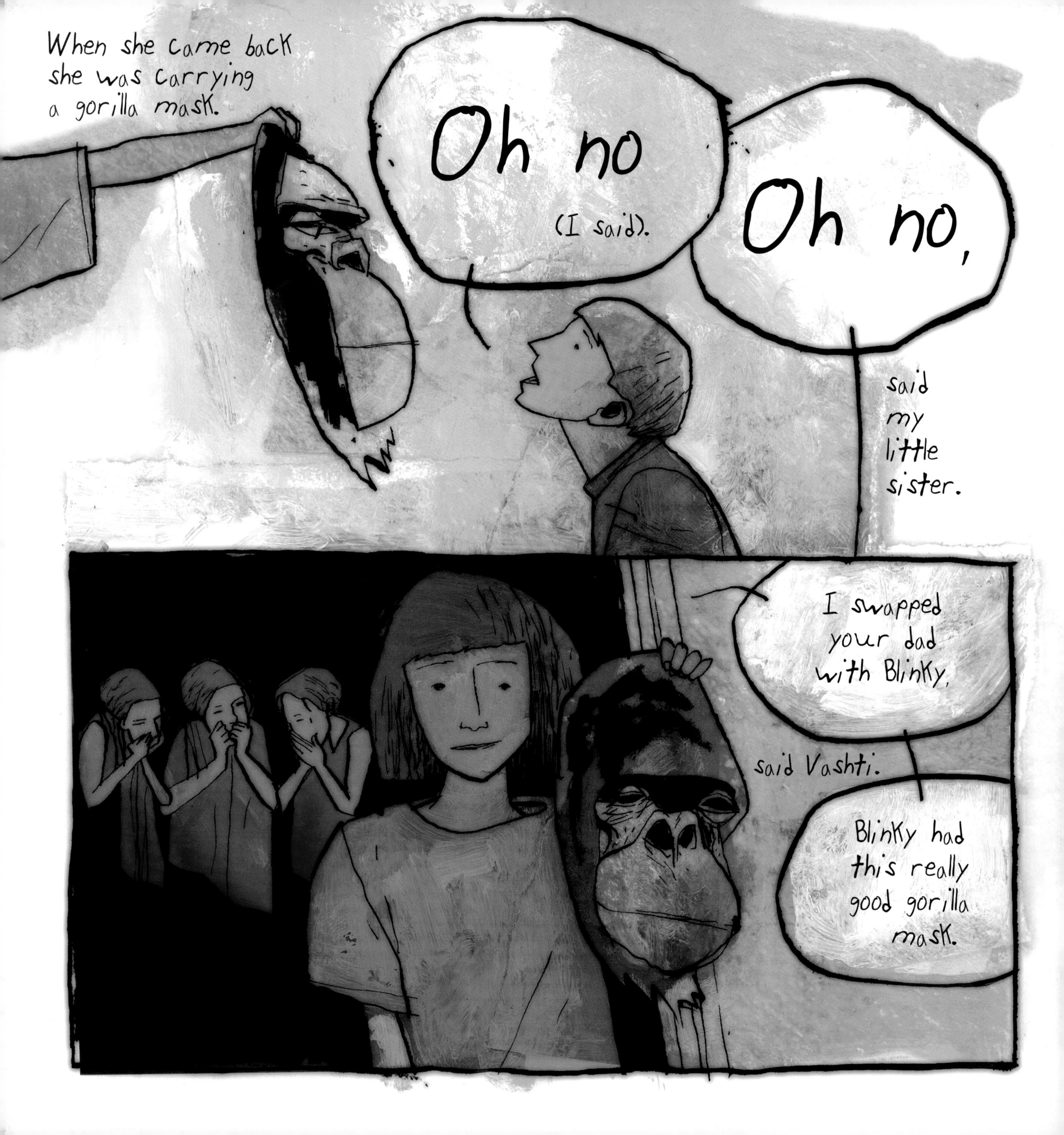
When she came back she was carrying a gorilla mask.
Oh no (I said).
Oh no,
said my little sister.
I swapped your dad with Blinky,
said Vashti.
Blinky had this really good gorilla mask.

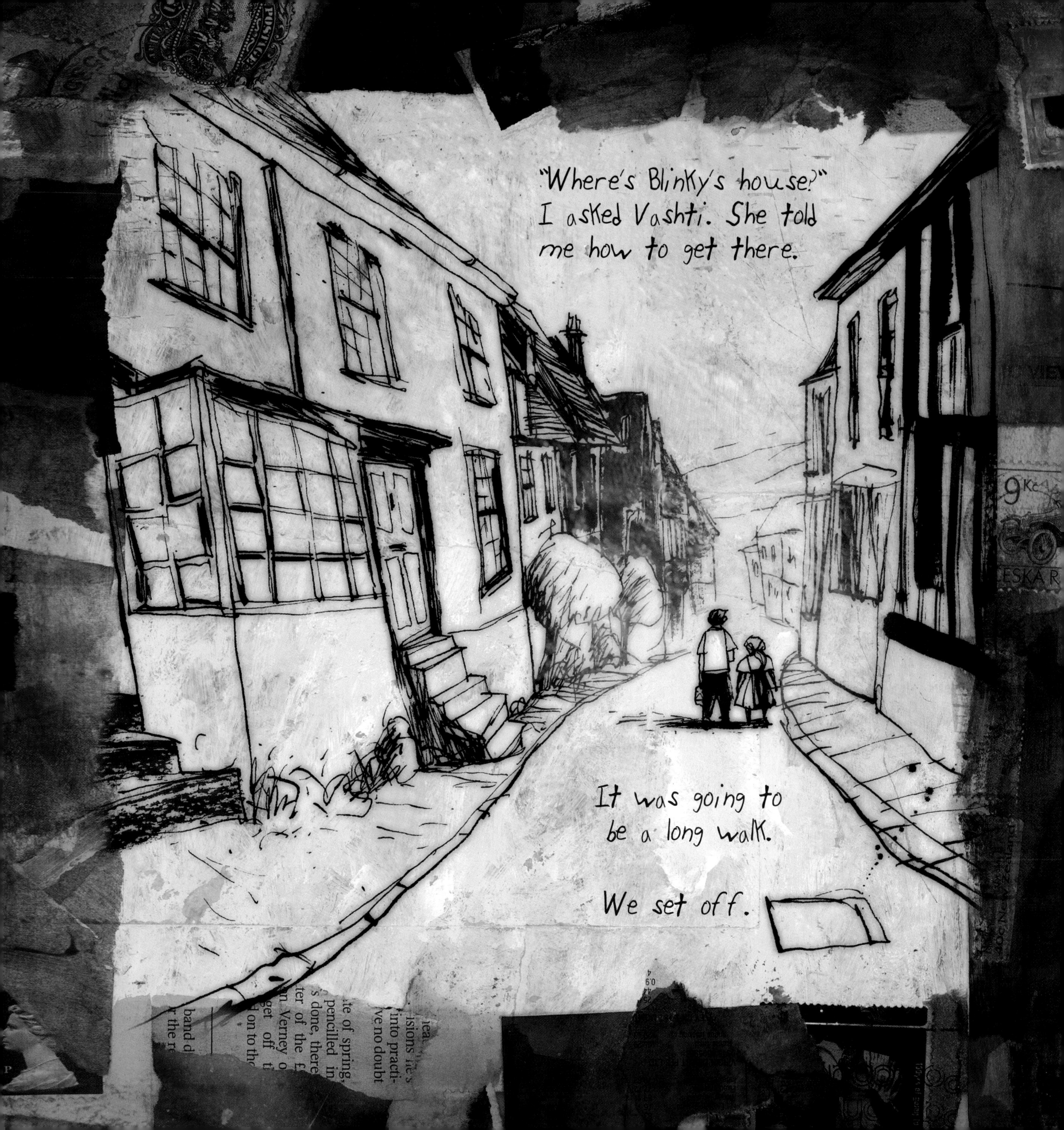
"Where's Blinky's house?" I asked Vashti. She told me how to get there.
It was going to be a long walk.
We set off.

"Can I put on the gorilla mask?" asked my little sister. "Okay," I said. She put on the gorilla mask.

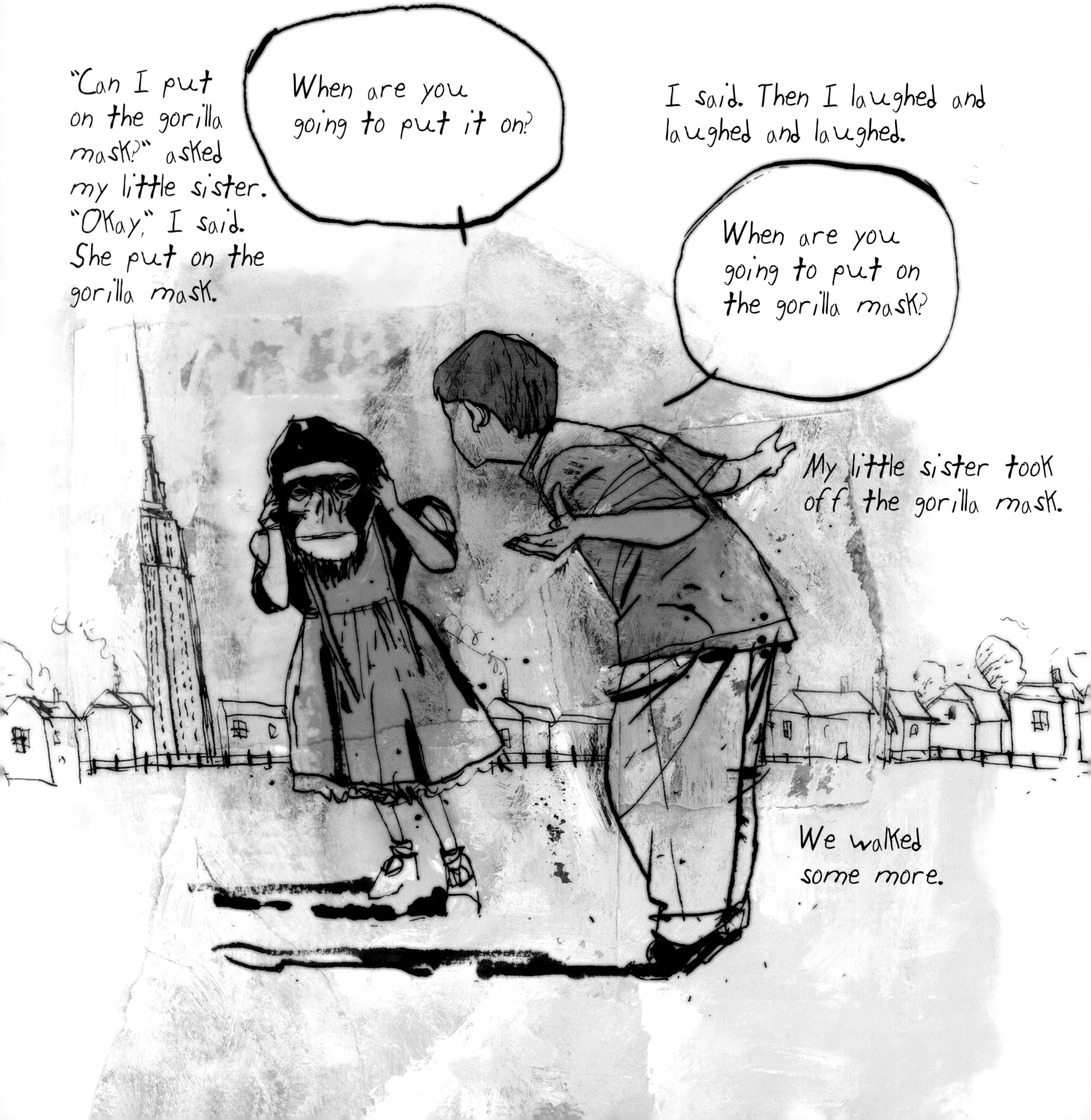
When are you going to put it on?
When are you going to put on the gorilla mask?

I said. Then I laughed and laughed and laughed.

My little sister took off the gorilla mask.

We walked some more.

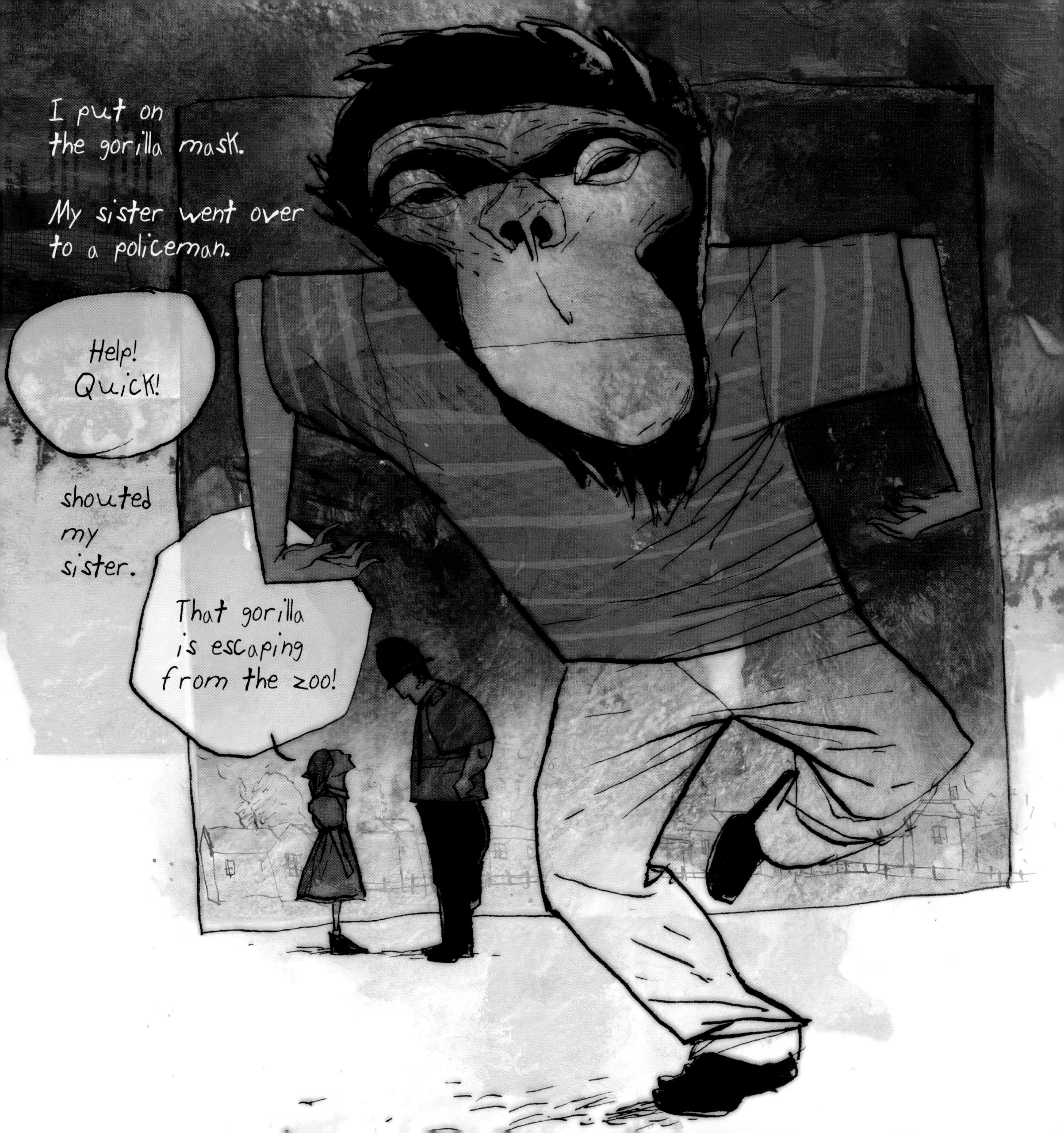
I put on the gorilla mask.
My sister went over to a policeman.
Help! QuicK!
shouted my sister.
That gorilla is escaping from the zoo!

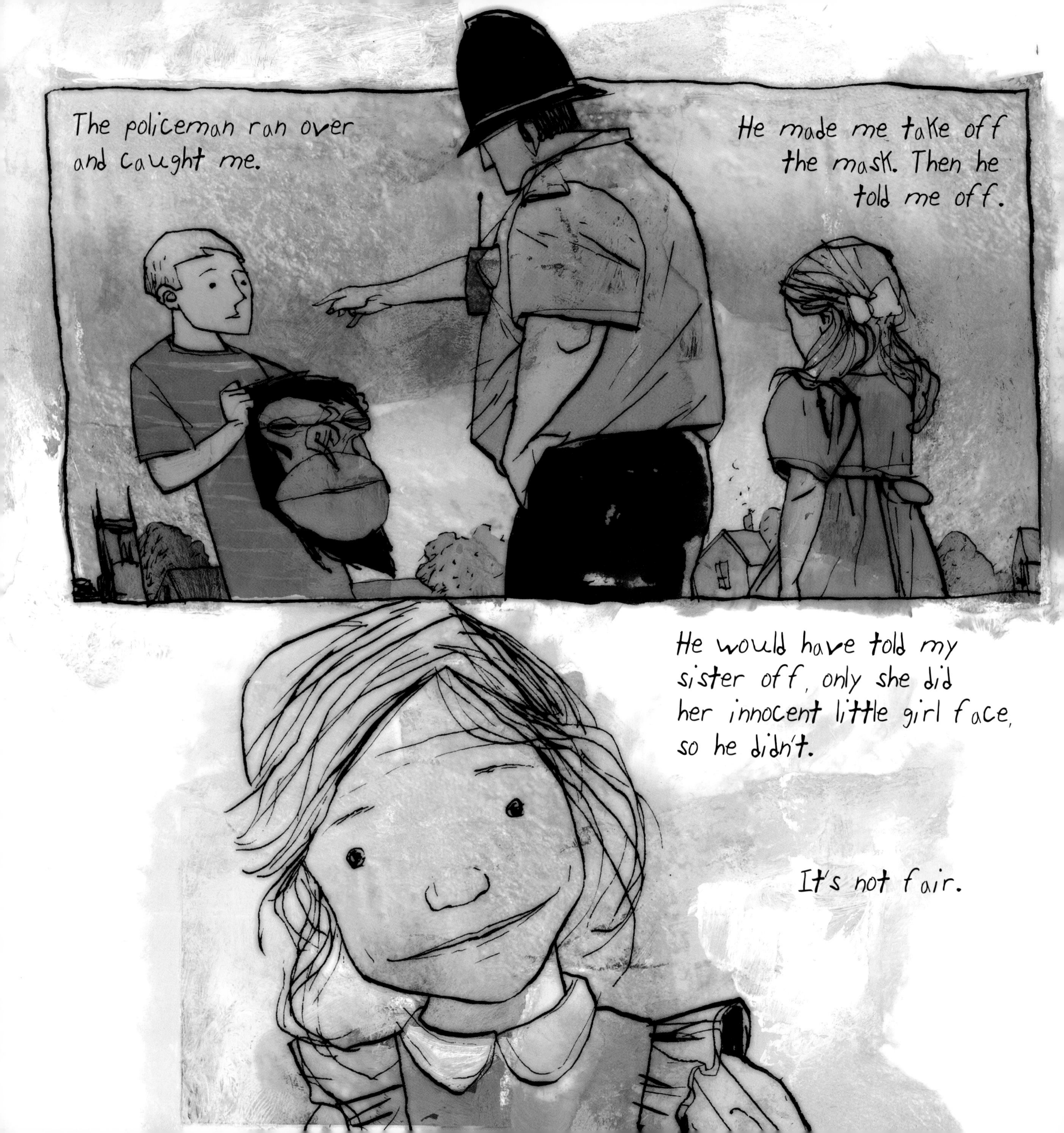
The policeman ran over and caught me.
He made me take off the mask. Then he told me off.
He would have told my sister off, only she did her innocent little girl face, so he didn't.
It's not fair.

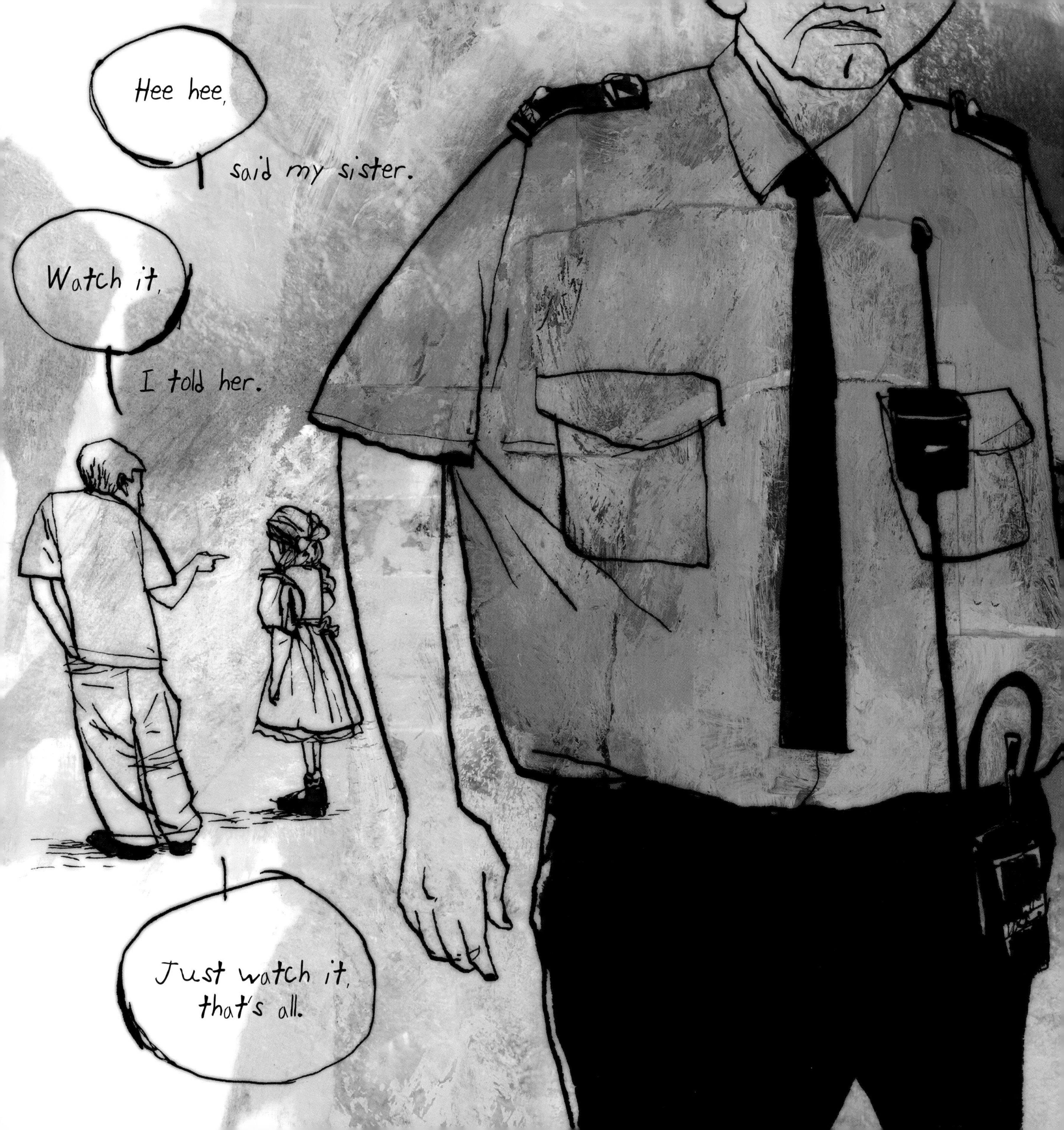
Hee hee,
said my sister.
Watch it,
I told her.
Just watch it, that's all.

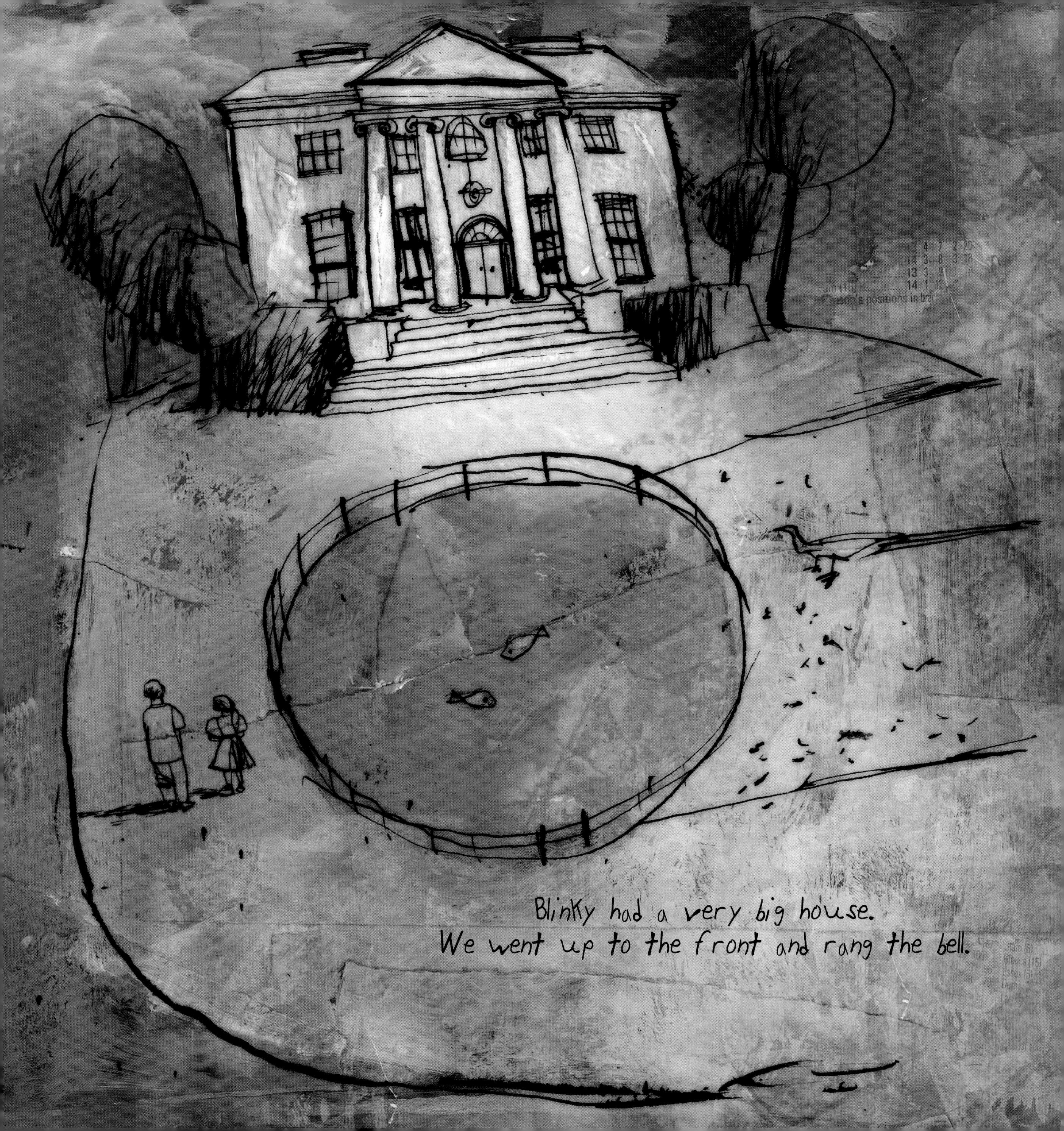

Blinky had a very big house.
We went up to the front and rang the bell.

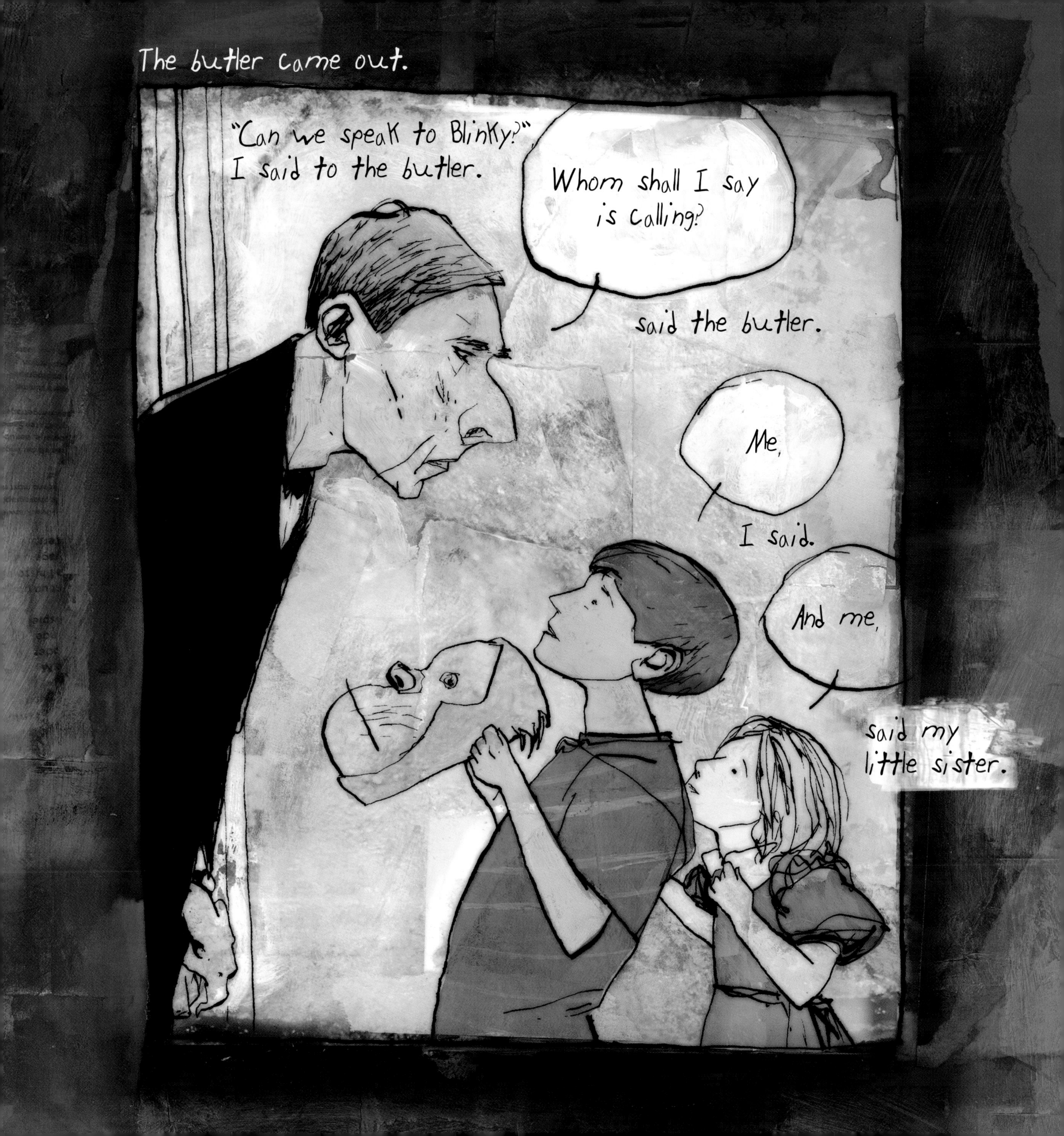
The butler came out.
"Can we speak to Blinky?", I said to the butler.
Whom shall I say is calling?
said the butler.
Me,
I said.
And me,
said my little sister.

Blinky came down the big stairs. He looked very pleased to see the gorilla mask.

"Are you bringing it back?" he asked.

"Yes we are," I told him.

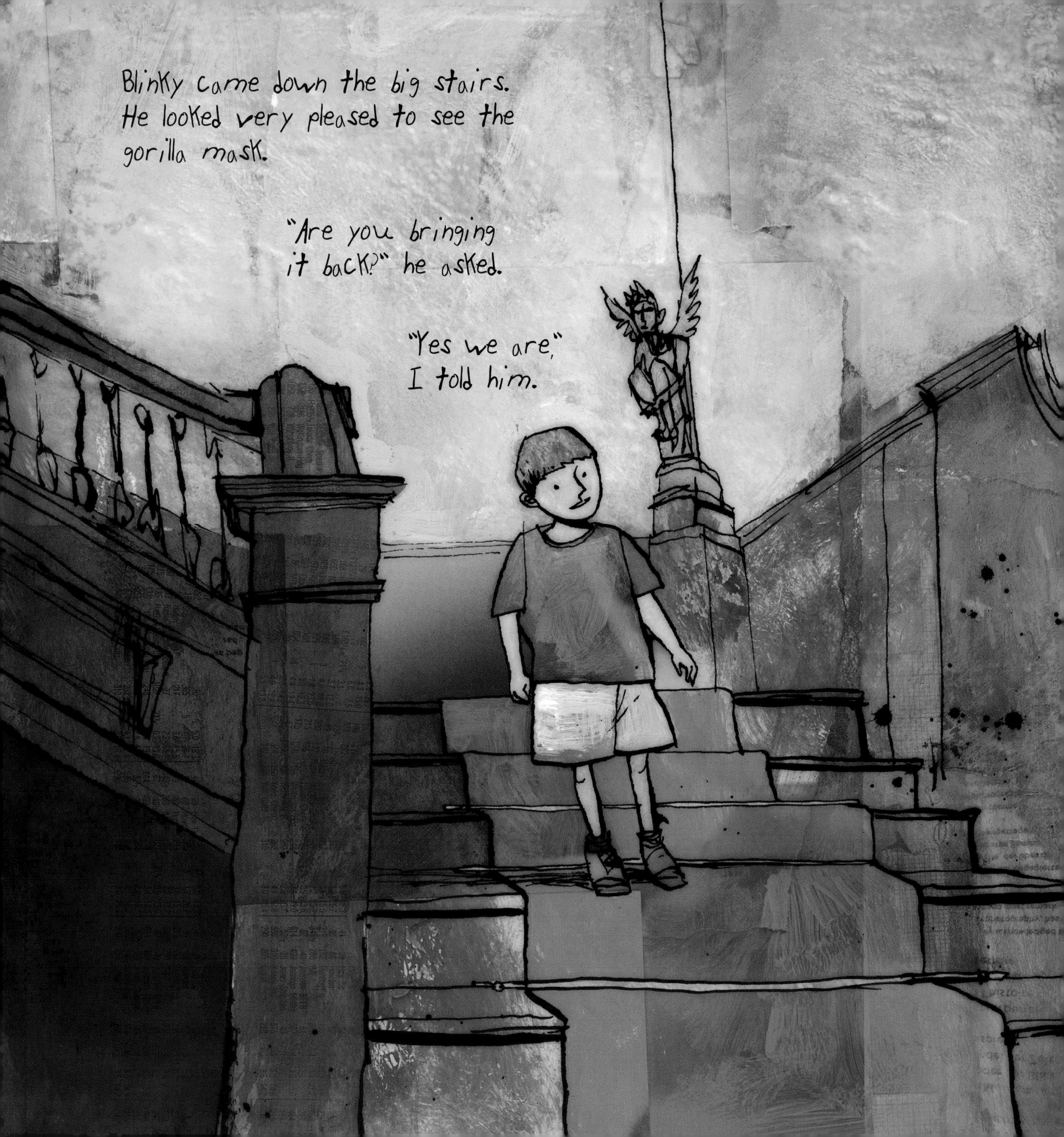

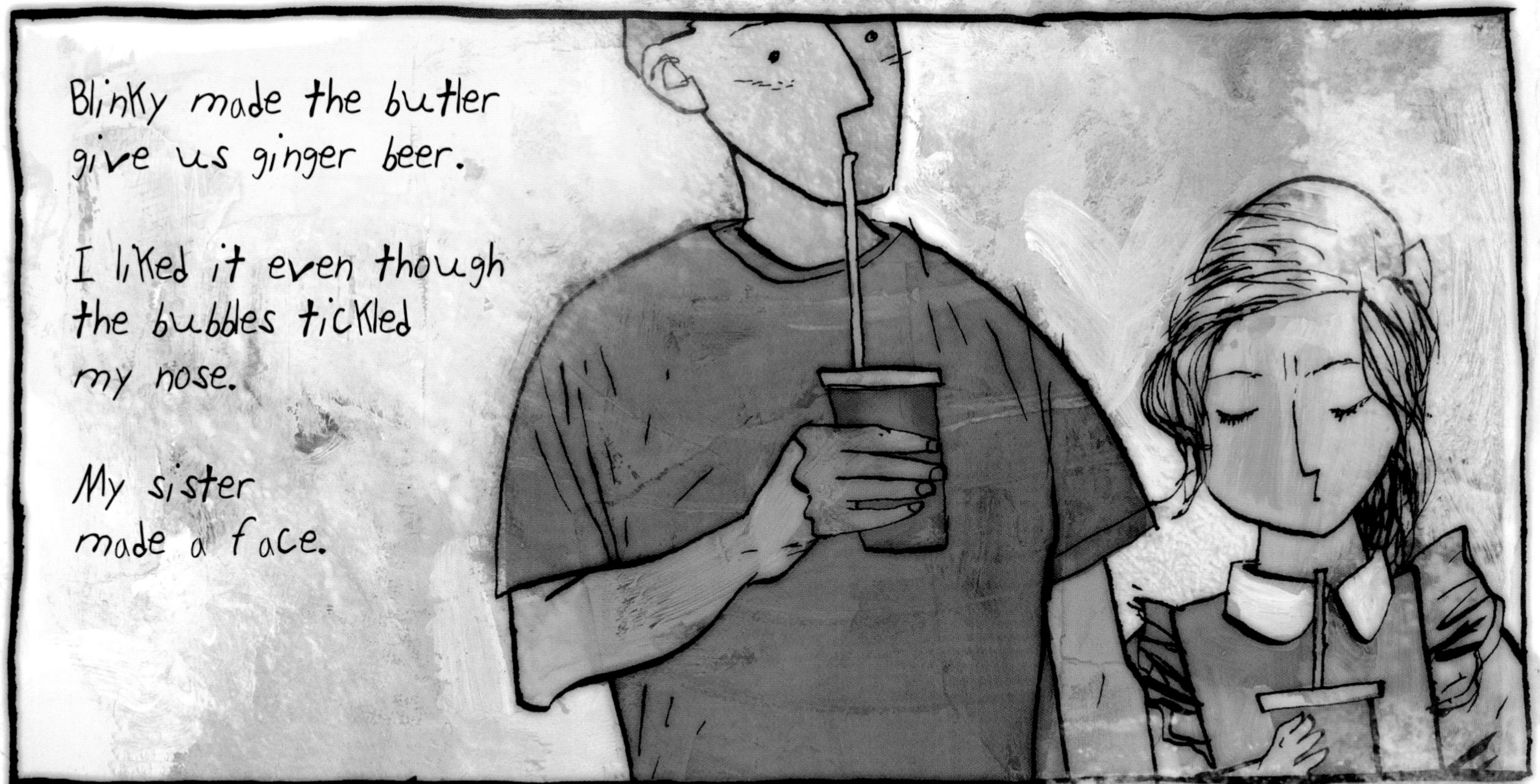
Blinky made the butler give us ginger beer.
I liked it even though the bubbles tickled my nose.
My sister made a face.
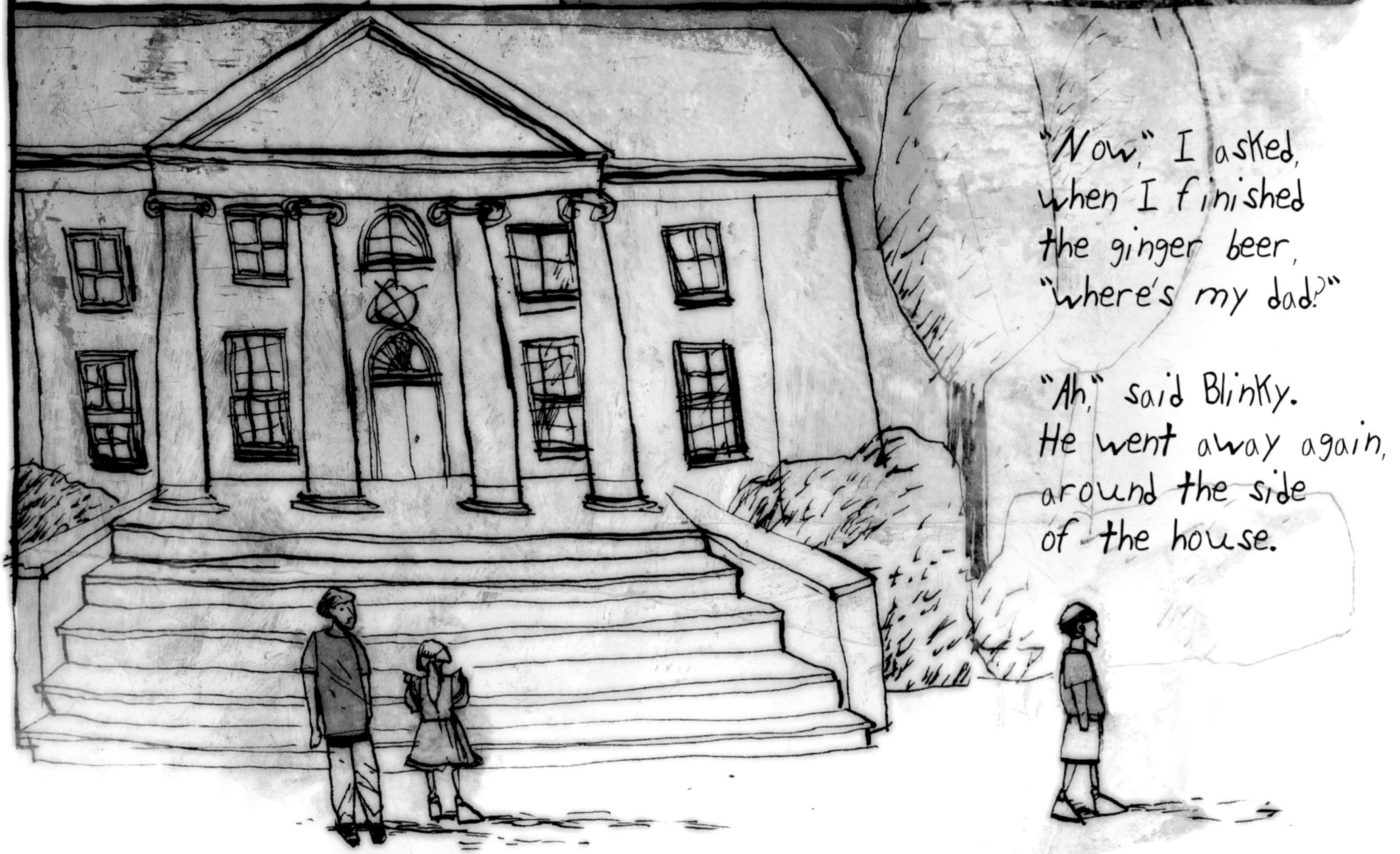
"Now," I asked, when I finished the ginger beer, "where's my dad?"
"Ah," said Blinky. He went away again, around the side of the house.

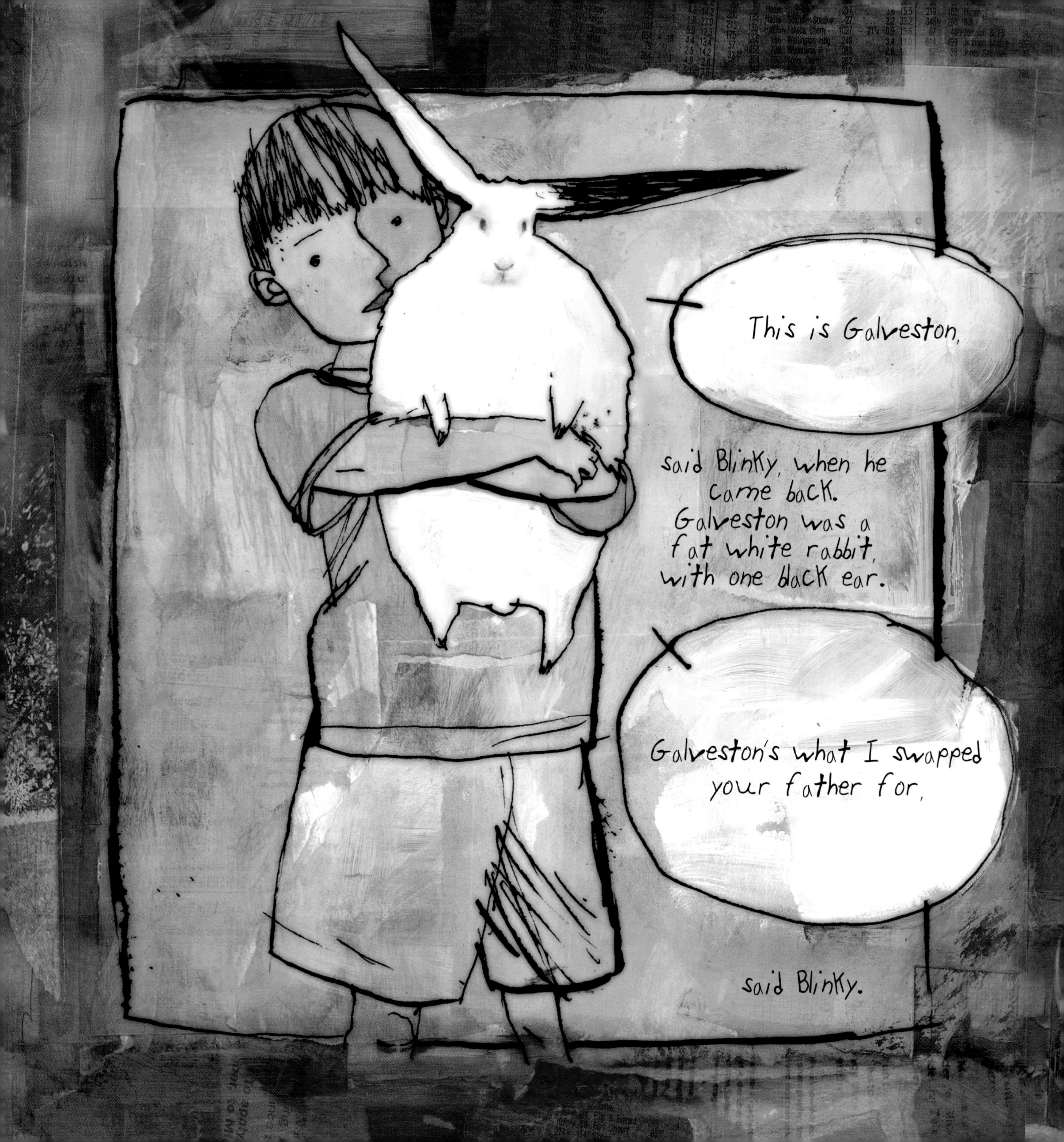
This is Galveston,
said Blinky, when he came back. Galveston was a fat white rabbit, with one black ear.
Galveston's what I swapped your father for,
said Blinky.

I gave him the gorilla mask. He gave me Galveston and a map he drew of how to get to Patti's house.

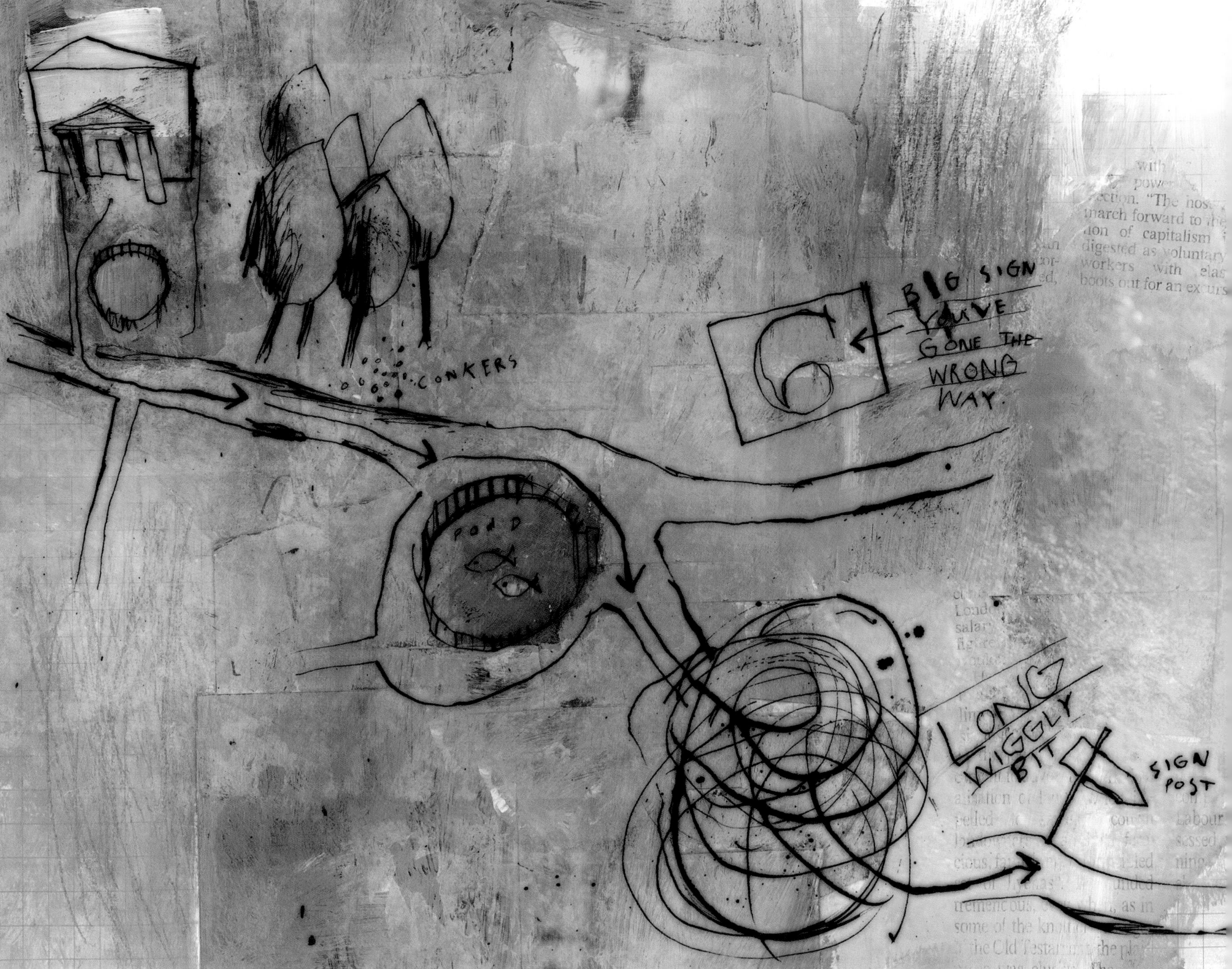
CONKERS
BIG SIGN
YOU'VE GONE THE WRONG WAY.
POND
LONG WIGGLY BIT
SIGN POST

I'd never walked so far in my whole life.

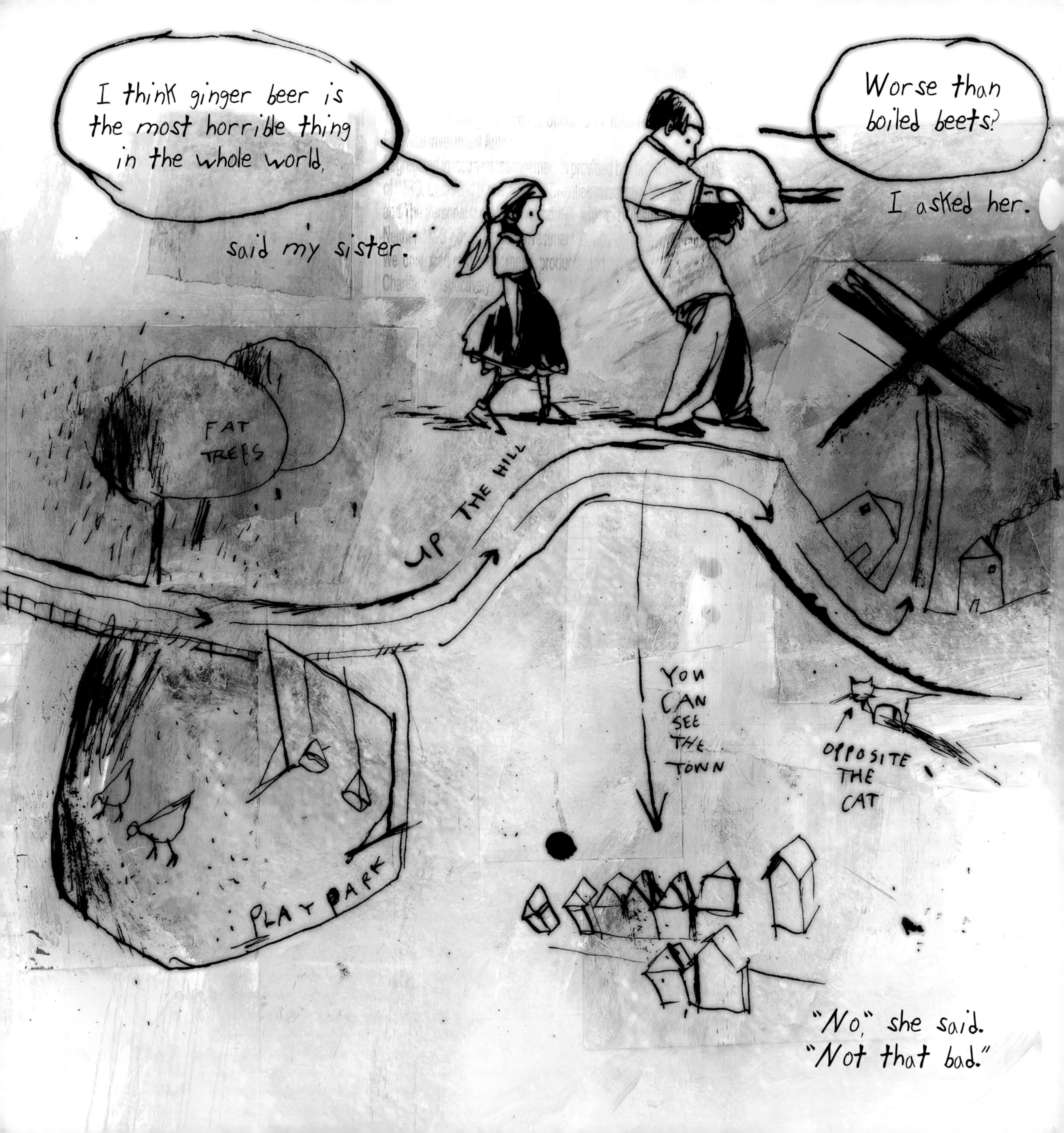
I think ginger beer is the most horrible thing in the whole world,
said my sister.
Worse than boiled beets?
I asked her.
FAT TREES
UP THE HILL
YOU CAN SEE THE TOWN
OPPOSITE THE CAT
PLAY PARK
"No," she said. "Not that bad."

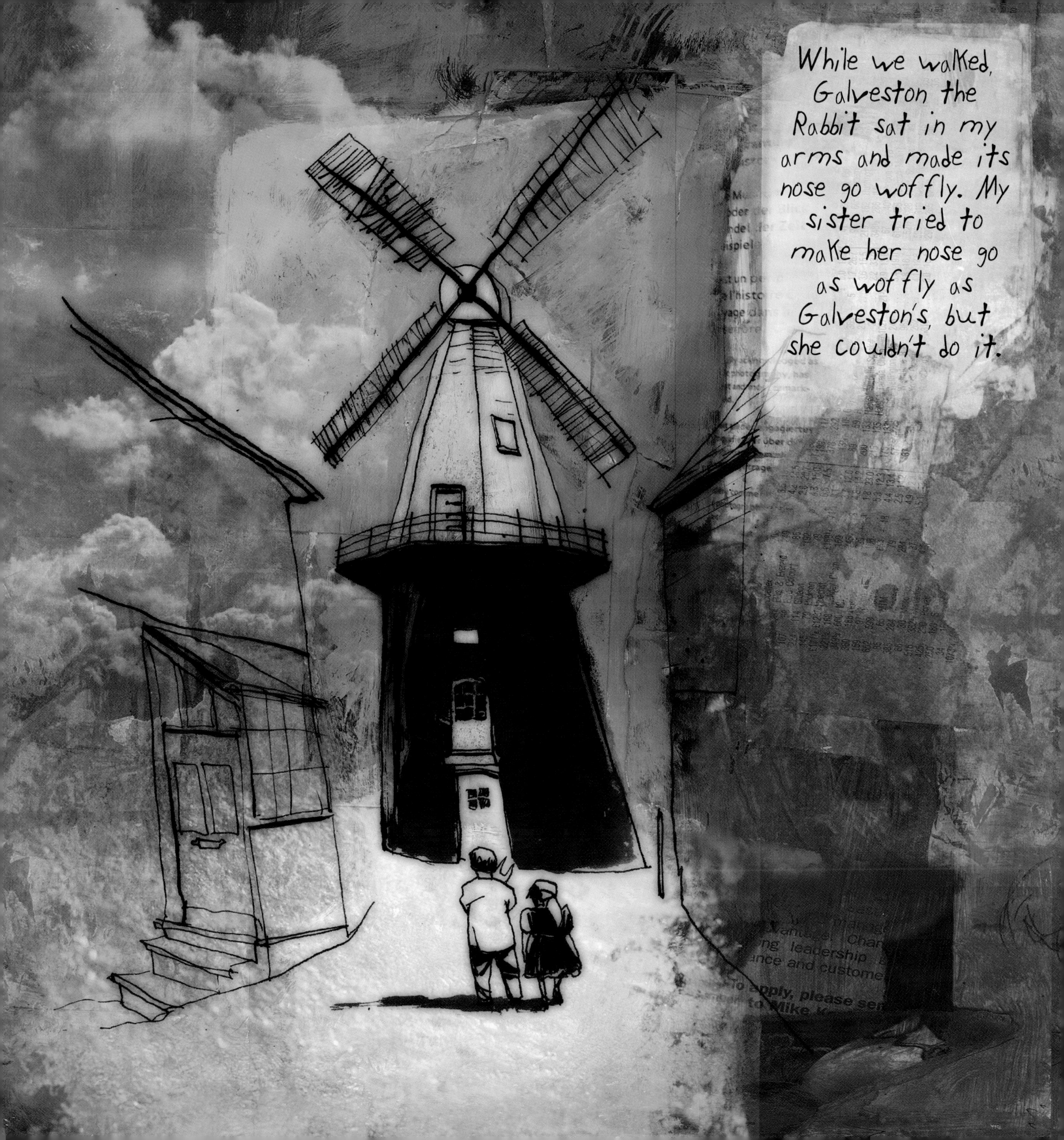

While we walked, Galveston the Rabbit sat in my arms and made its nose go woffly. My sister tried to make her nose go as woffly as Galveston's, but she couldn't do it.

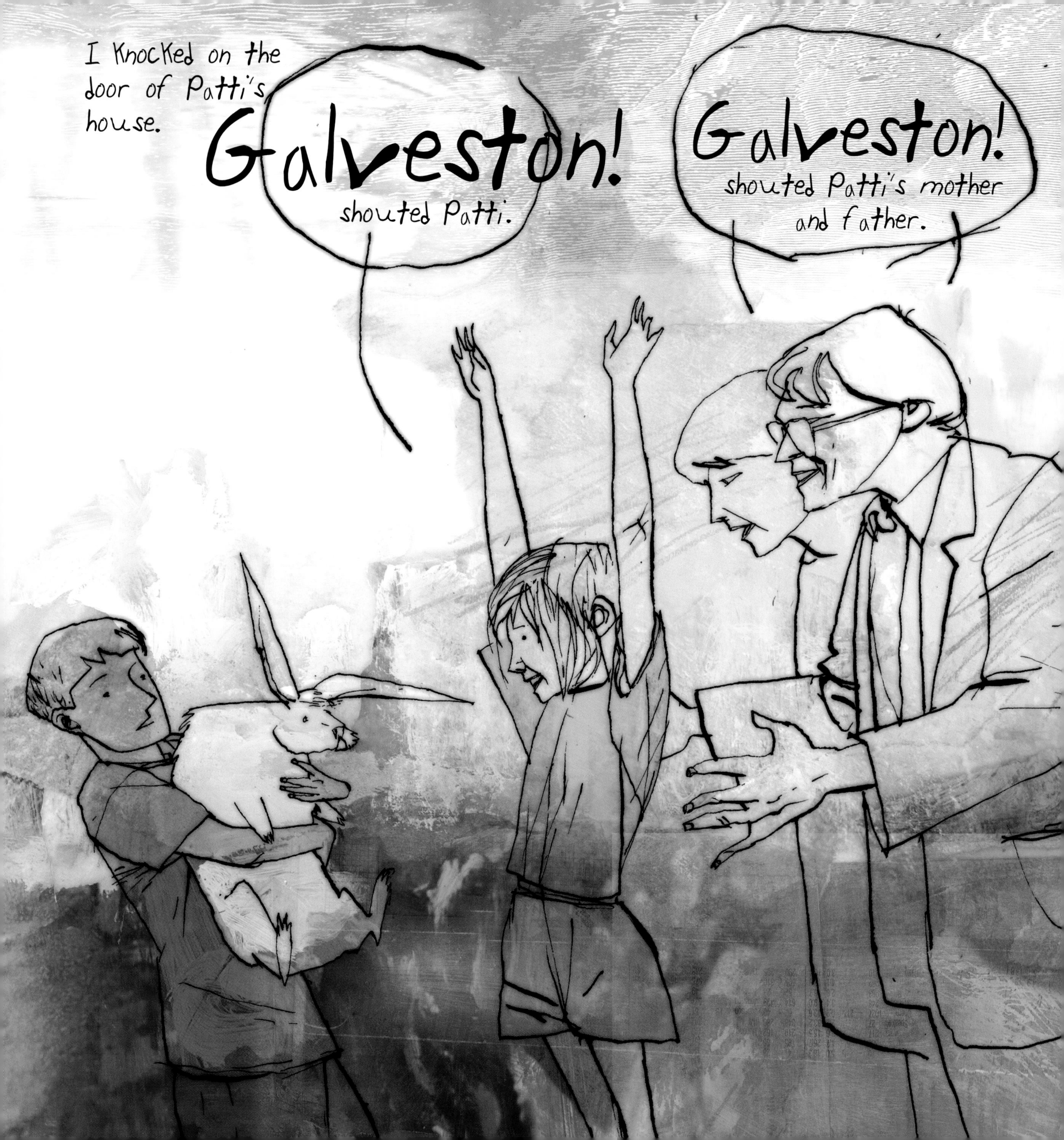
I knocked on the door of Patti's house.
Galveston! shouted Patti.
Galveston! shouted Patti's mother and father.

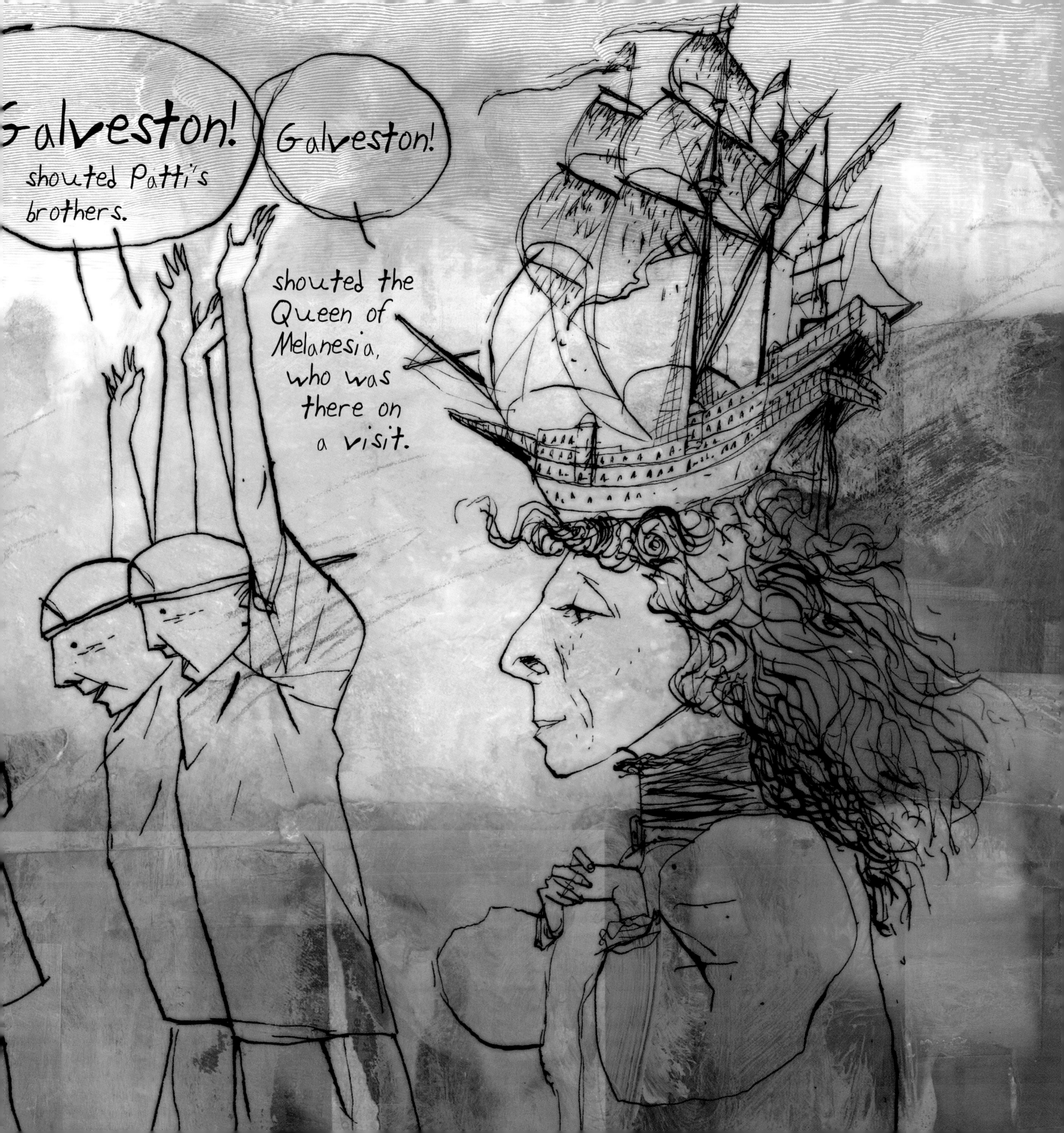
Galveston! shouted Patti's brothers.
Galveston!
shouted the Queen of Melanesia, who was there on a visit.

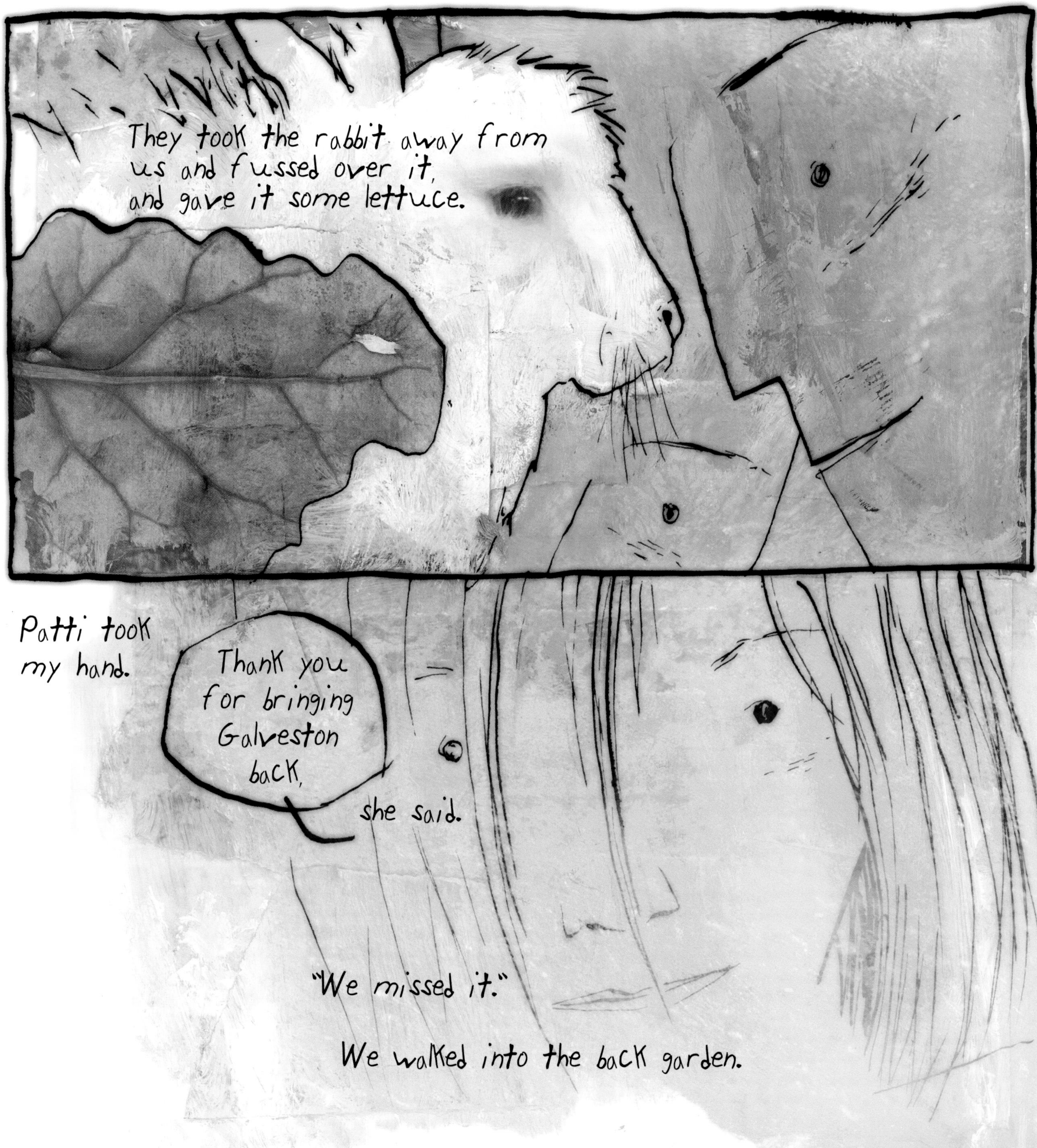

They took the rabbit away from us and fussed over it, and gave it some lettuce.
Patti took my hand.
Thank you for bringing Galveston back,
she said.
"We missed it."
We walked into the back garden.

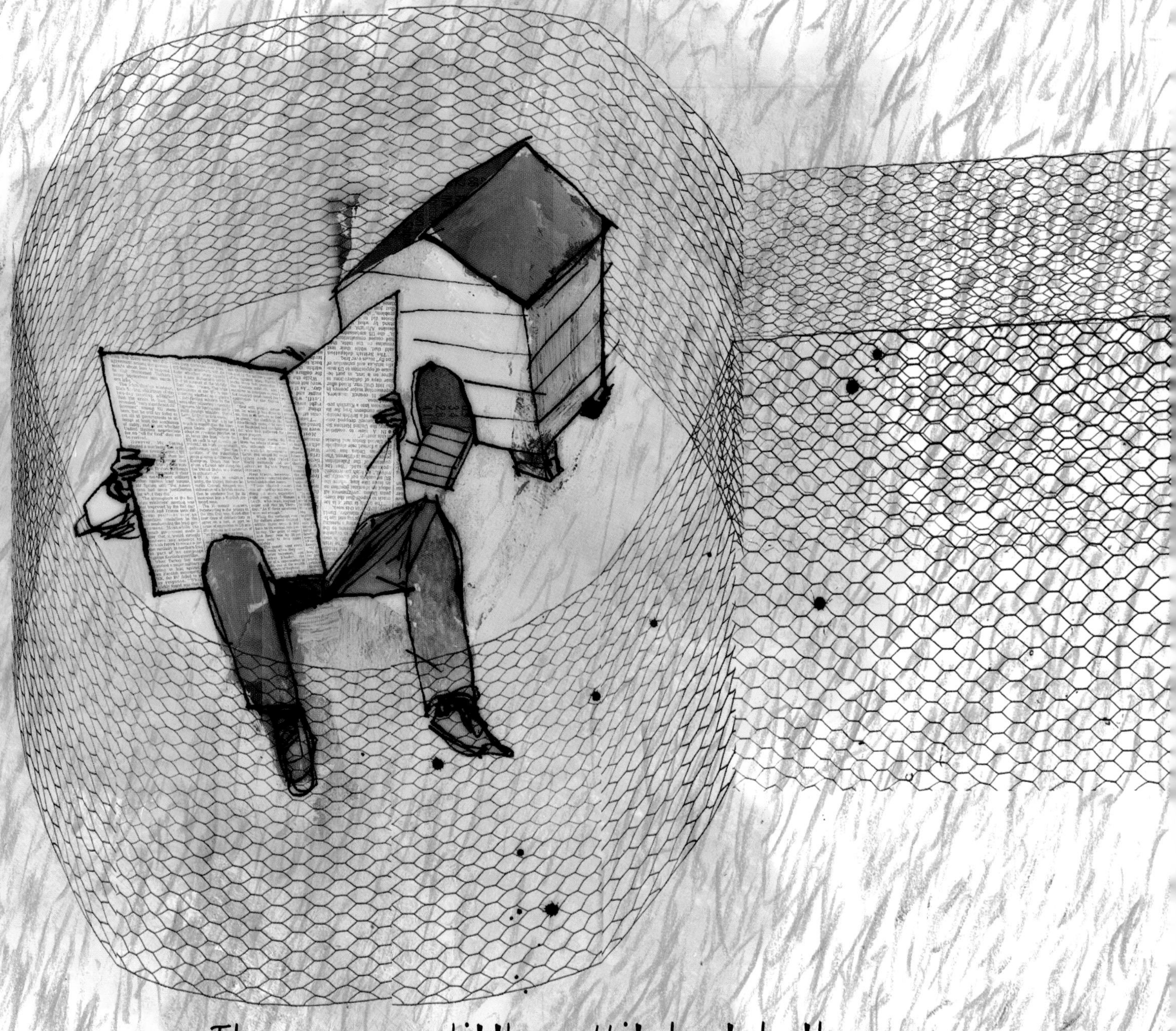

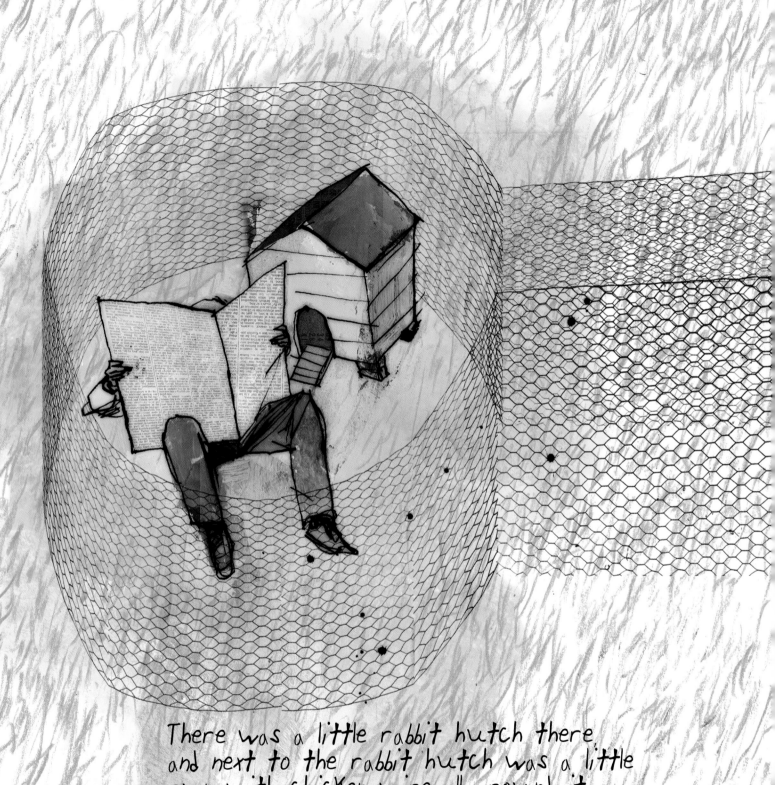

There was a little rabbit hutch there, and next to the rabbit hutch was a little run with chicken wire all around it. My dad sat on the grass, in the chicken wire run, reading his newspaper and eating a carrot. He looked a bit lonely, and he had grass all over his trousers.

"Come on, Dad," I said, and I opened the gate in the chicken wire.

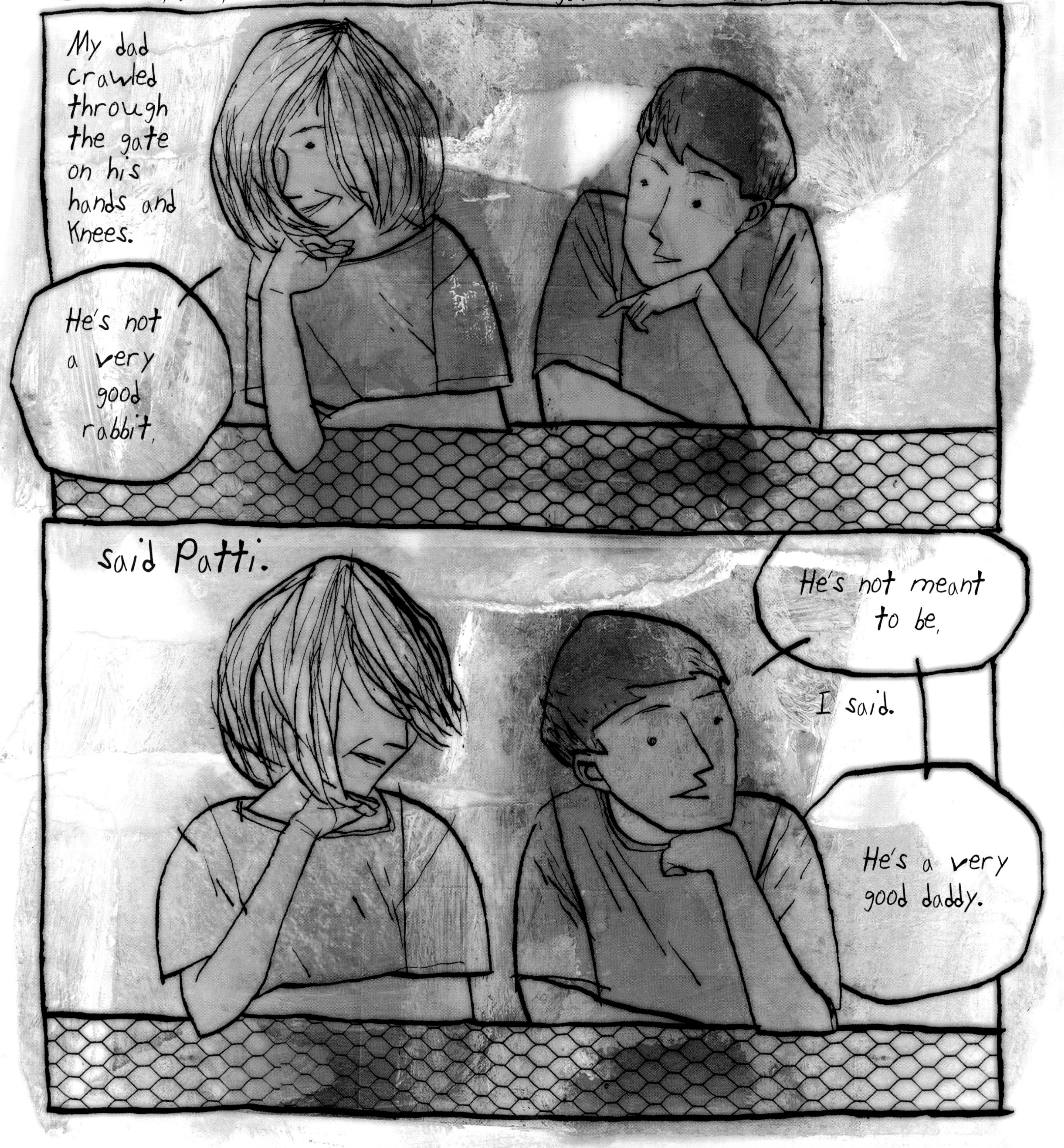
My dad crawled through the gate on his hands and knees.
He's not a very good rabbit,
said Patti.
He's not meant to be,
I said.
He's a very good daddy.

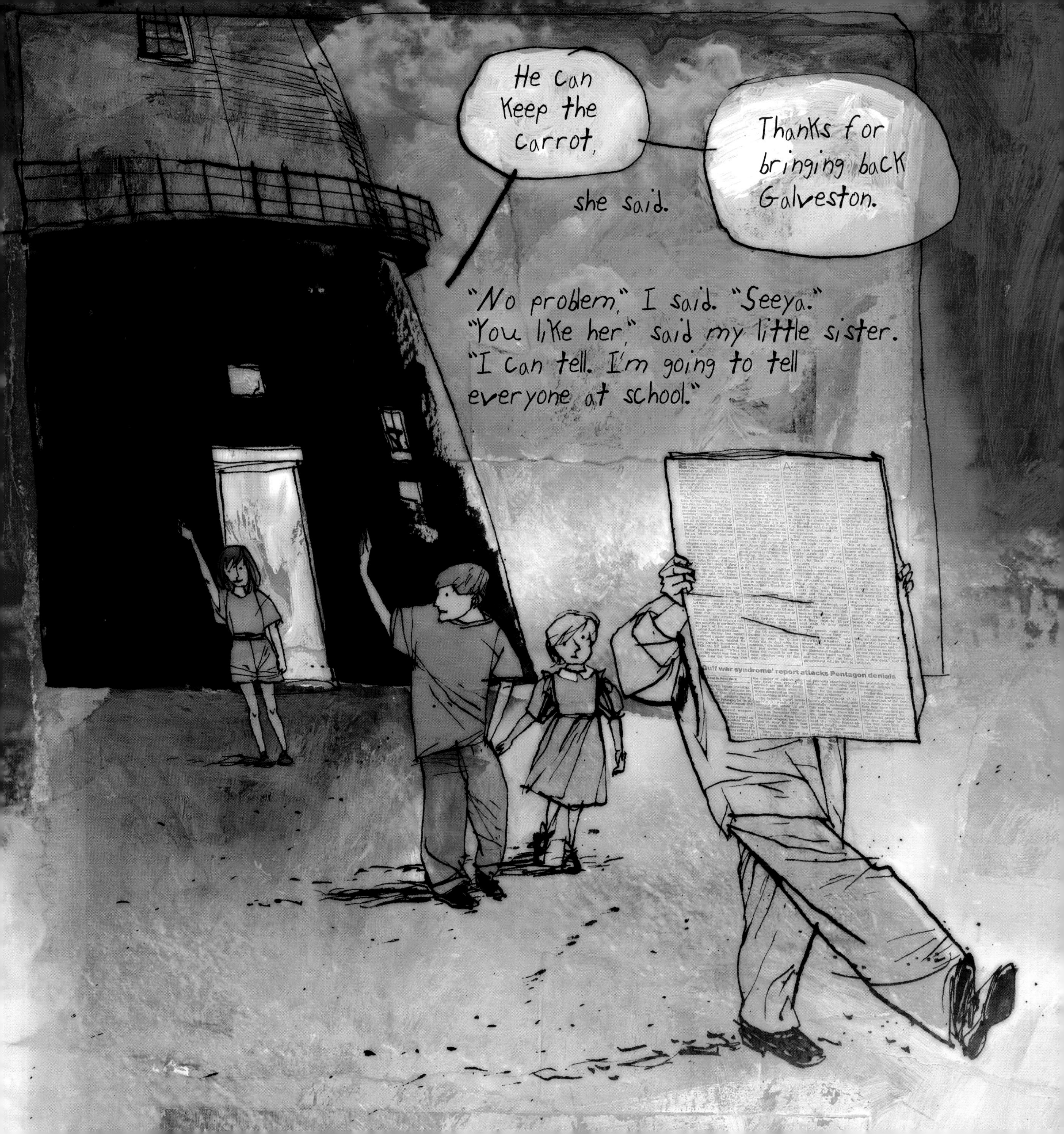
He can Keep the carrot,
she said.
Thanks for bringing back Galveston.
"No problem," I said. "Seeya."
"You like her," said my little sister.
"I can tell. I'm going to tell everyone at school."
Gulf war syndrome' report attacks Pentagon denials

Last week my little sister told everyone at school that I was adopted. The week before she told everyone at school that I was a space alien pretending to be me.

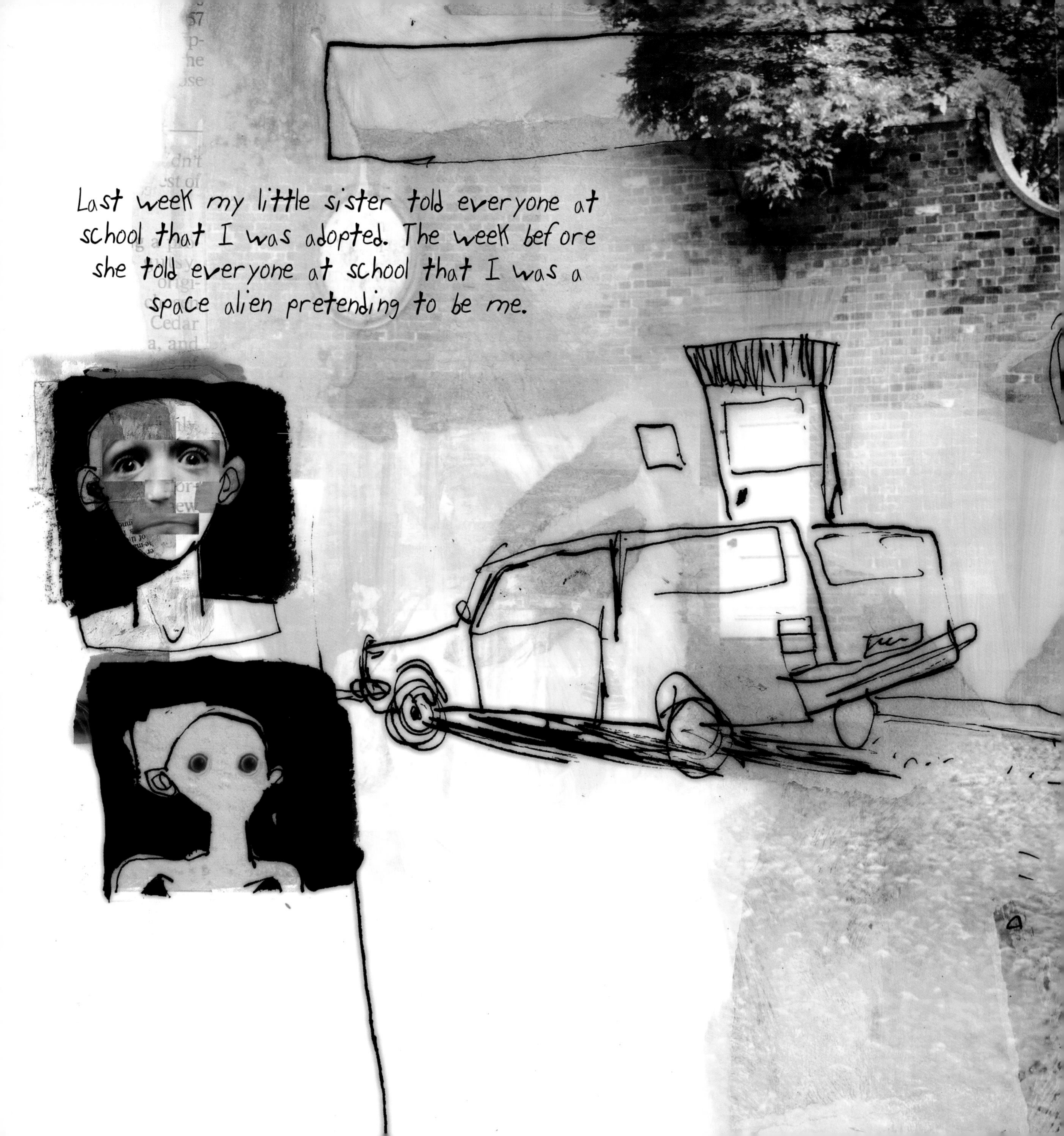

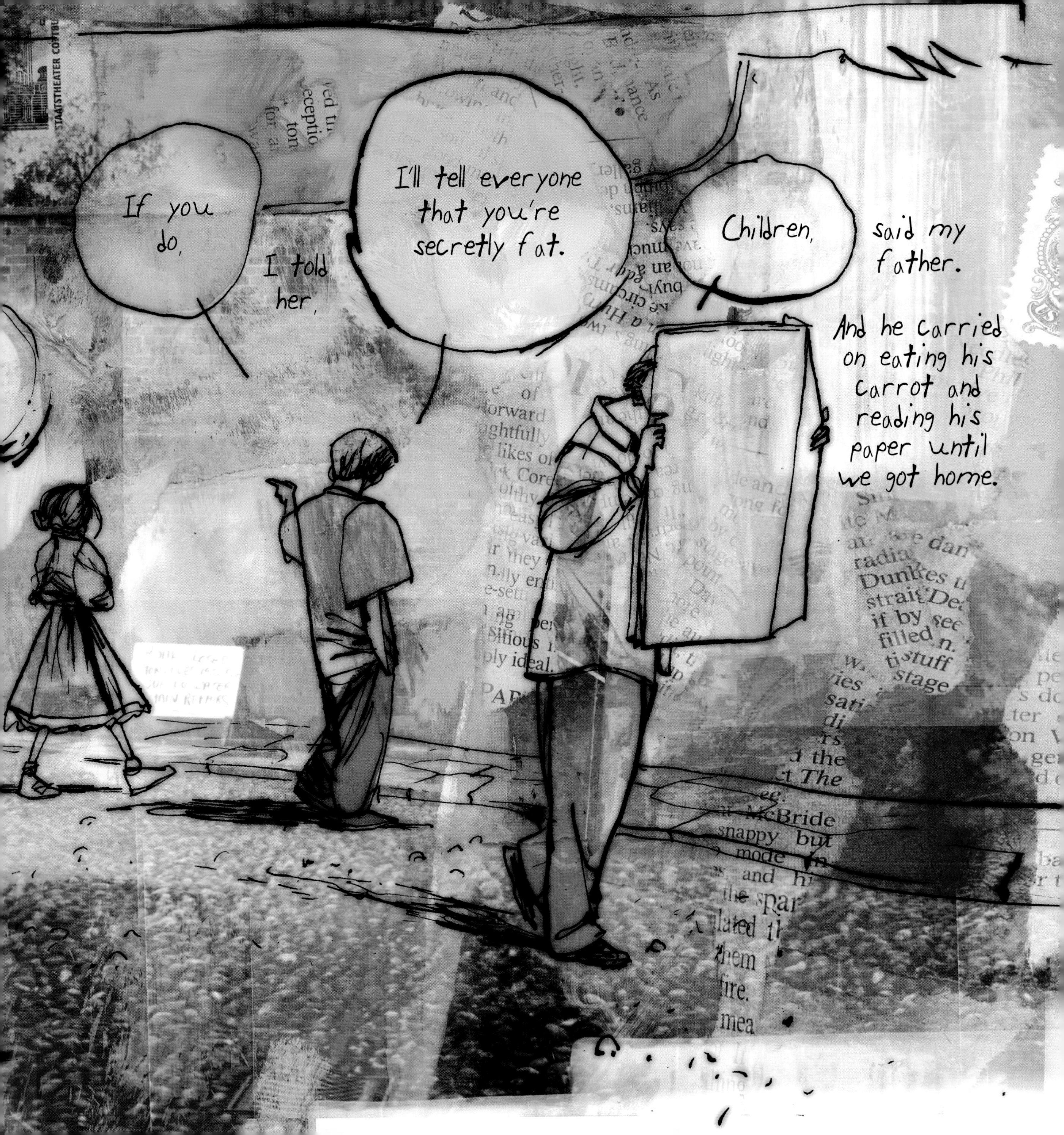
If you do,
I told her,
I'll tell everyone that you're secretly fat.
Children,
said my father.
And he carried on eating his carrot and reading his paper until we got home.

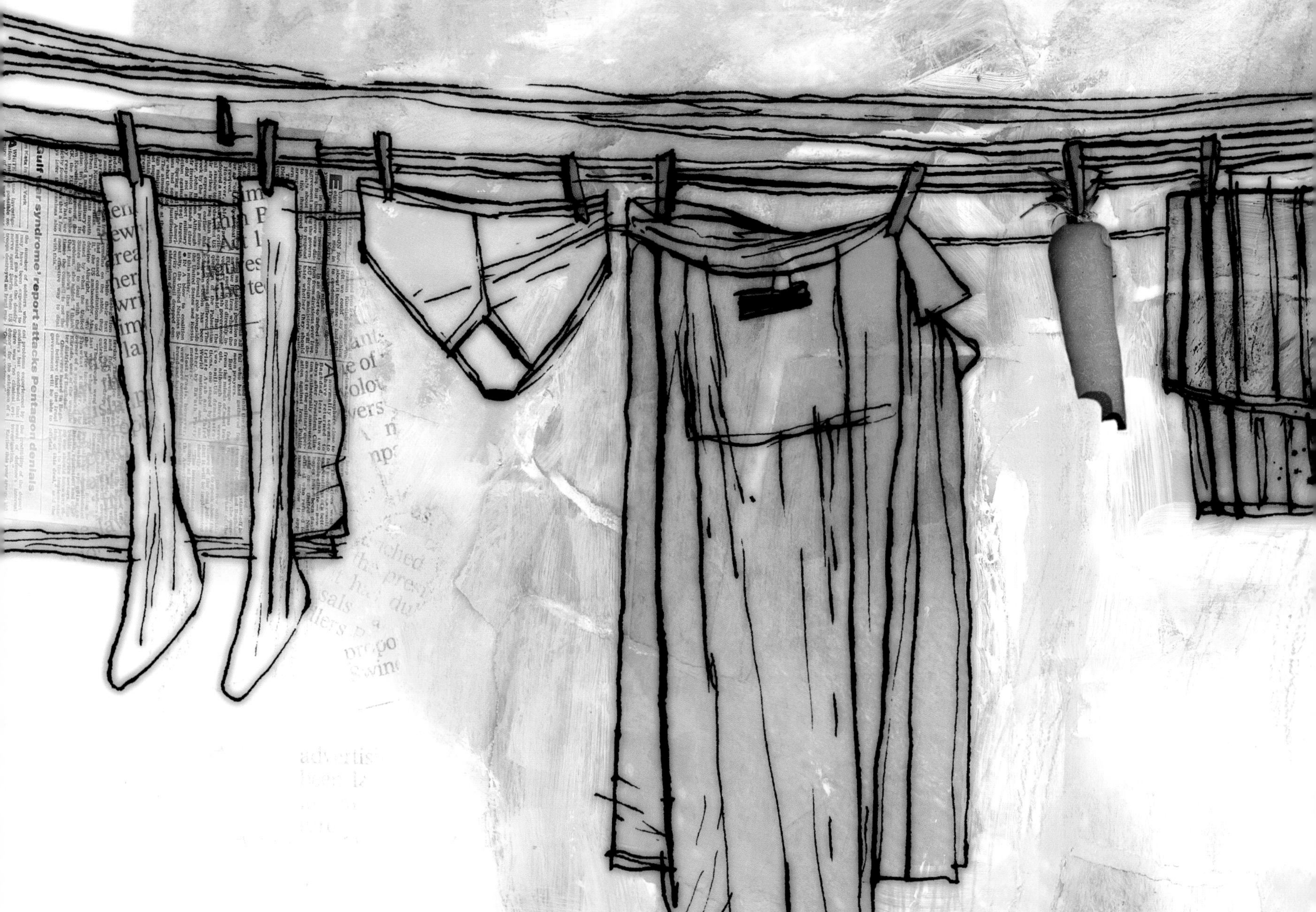

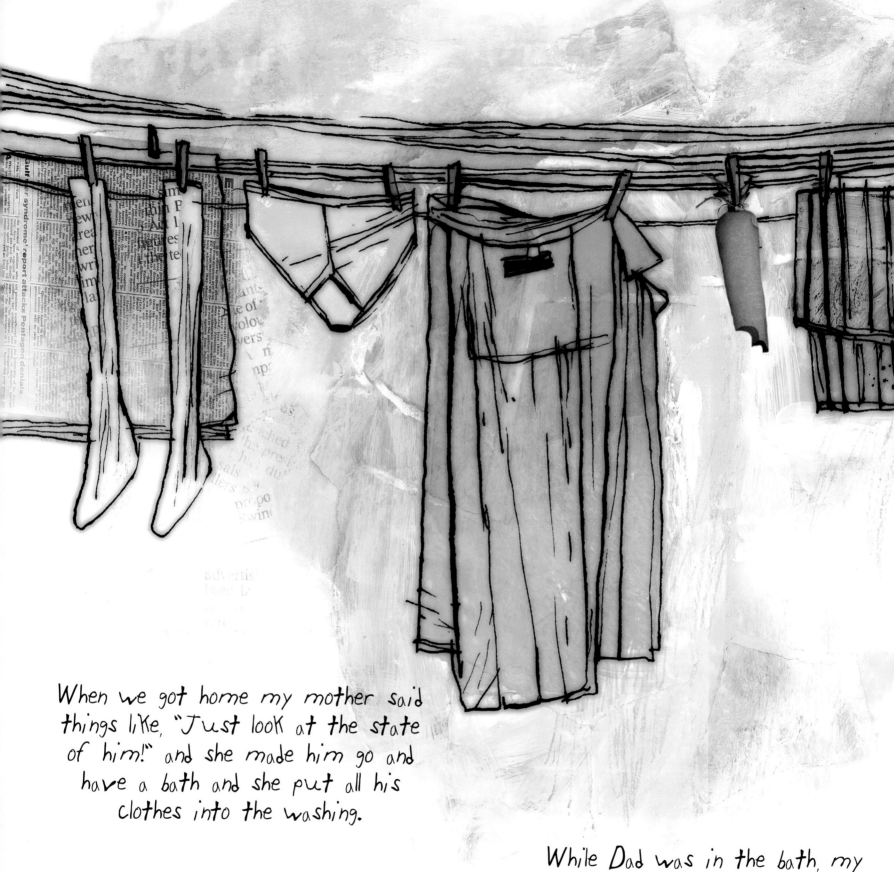

When we got home my mother said things like, "Just look at the state of him!" and she made him go and have a bath and she put all his clothes into the washing.

While Dad was in the bath, my mother told me off.

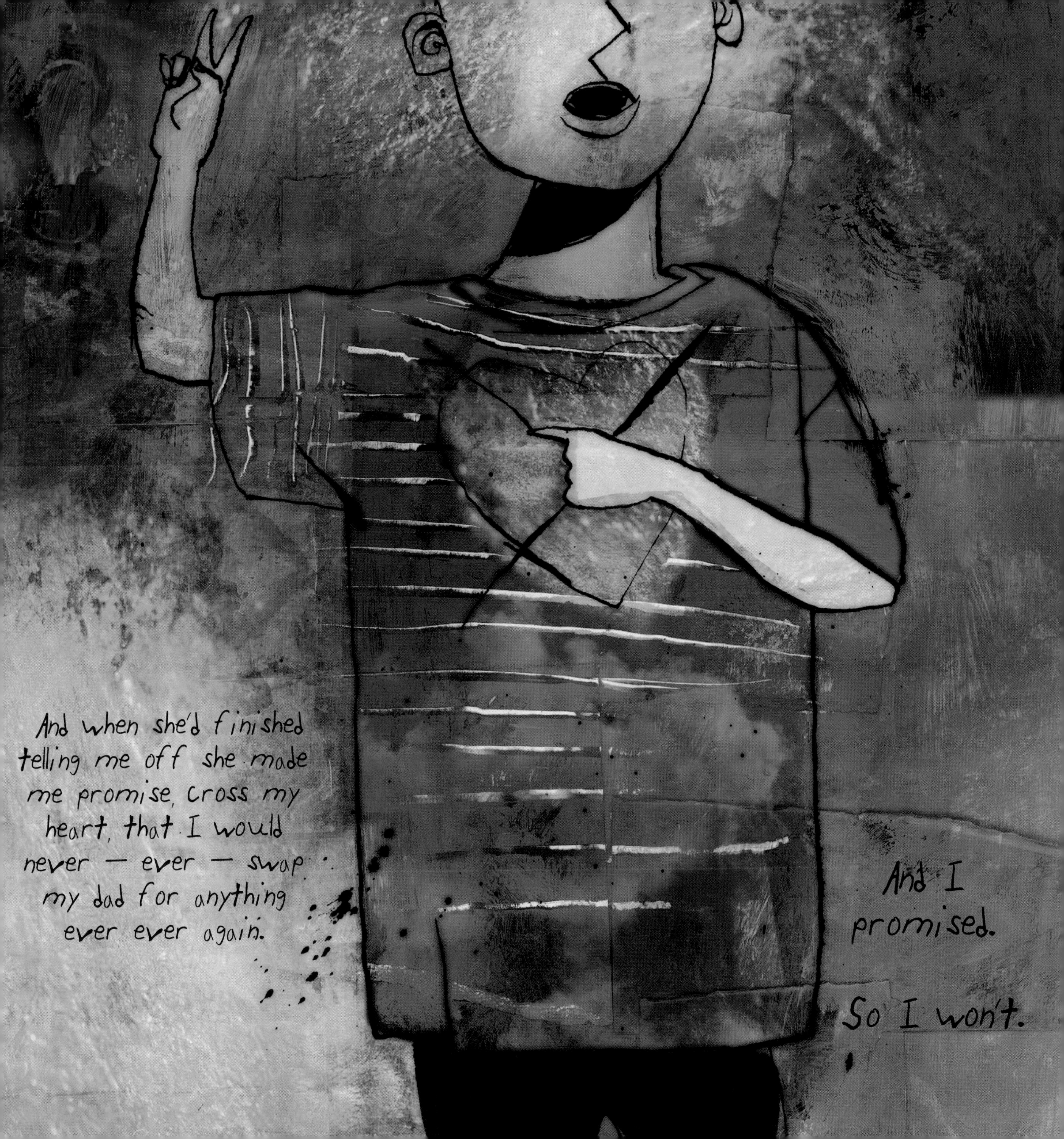

And when she'd finished telling me off she made me promise, cross my heart, that I would never — ever — swap my dad for anything ever ever again.

And I promised.

So I won't.

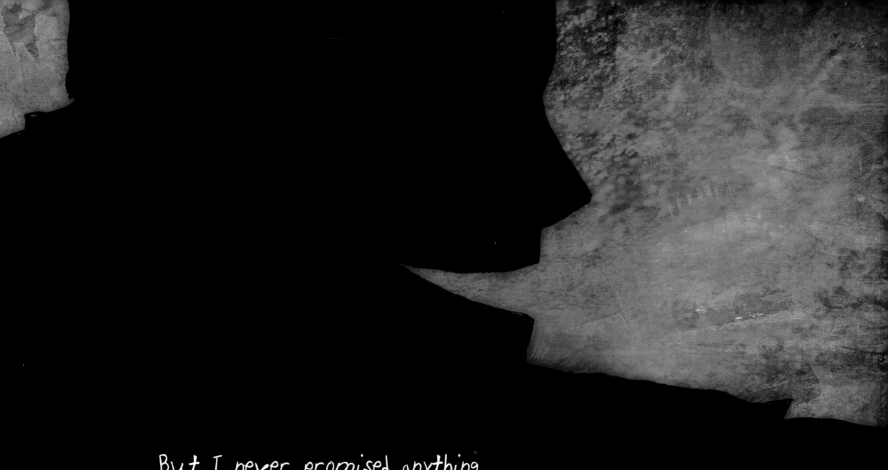

But I never promised anything
about my little sister. . . .

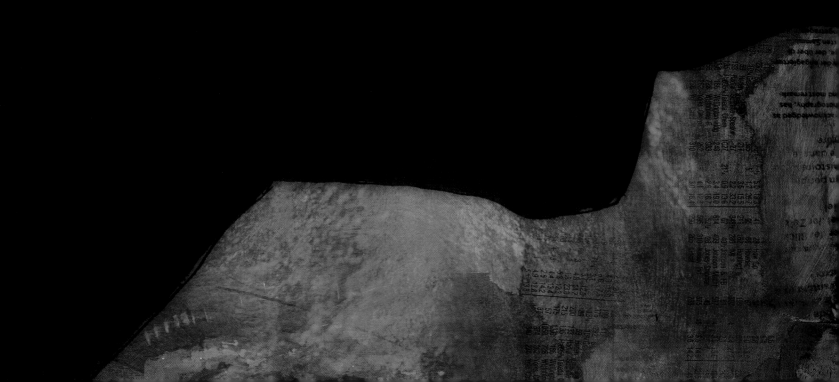

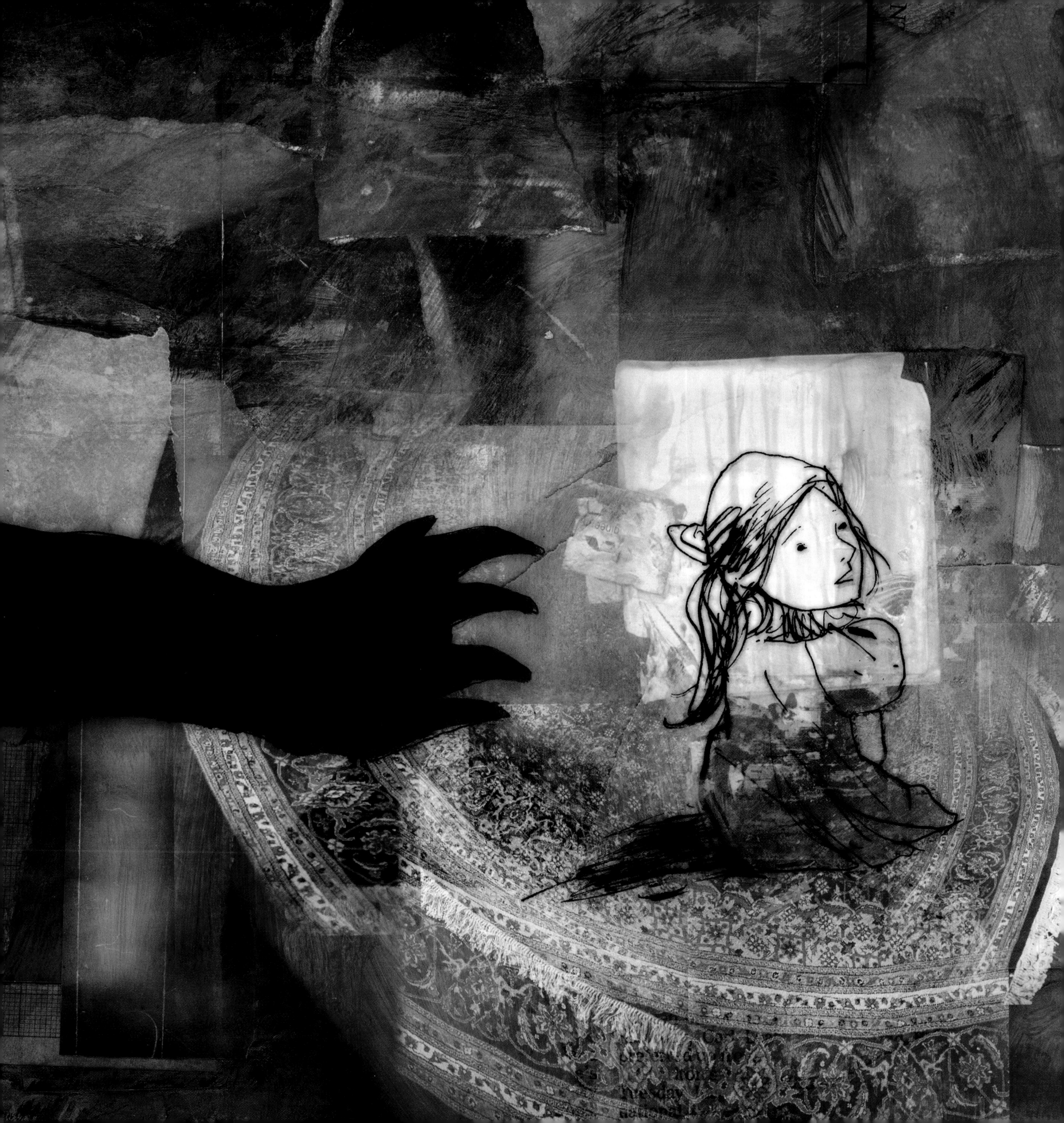

fin

Afterword

This book started like this.

My son, who is called Michael or Mike these days, but was Mikey back then, was angry at me. I'd said one of those things that parents say, like "isn't it time you were in bed," and he had looked up at me, furious, and said, "I wish I didn't have a dad! I wish I had . . ." and then he stopped and thought, trying to think of what one could have instead of a father. Finally he said, "I wish I had goldfish!"

And he stomped off to bed.

I was awed by the idea. Of course one ought to be able to trade a father for goldfish. It seemed a very sensible thing to do.

I wrote the first sentence or two on my computer and then wasn't quite sure how it went after that, so I stopped and did other things.

A few years later I was in a hotel in Galveston, Texas, where I had gone to write a television script. I was stuck on the script, so I looked at the files on my computer to see if there was anything there that was interesting—and waiting for me was the first sentence of that book I'd started about the boy who swapped his dad for two goldfish.

I knew what the next sentence was, so I wrote it. And the one after that. Eventually I'd finished a whole book (and I'd named a rabbit Galveston), and wasn't much further along with my television script.

I gave the book to Dave McKean, who drew the magical pictures.

The boy and his sister are a little bit Mike and his sister Holly, who spent the first dozen years of their lives locked in a bitter and deadly cold war, and a little bit me and my sister Claire, who, oddly enough, did exactly the same thing through most of our childhoods, but actually rather like each other these days. But mostly they are just themselves.

I always wanted a really convincing gorilla mask.

Neil Gaiman
October 17, 2003